HAND-ME-DOWN

Heartache

HAND-ME-DOWN *Heartache*

"Butler skillfully presents the world of Nina Lander, a recent college grad who goes on an odyssey of self-discovery."

—*Essence*

"Tajuana 'TJ' Butler is a hot new author. Don't miss her latest novel, *Hand-me-down Heartache*. It's a winner that you gotta check out!" —*Vivica A. Fox*

"Butler's second novel . . . deals sensitively with the impact of domestic abuse on an African-American family and the choices made by a young woman dealing with issues of self-doubt while seeking acceptance in her relationships."

—*Publishers Weekly*

"A novel of love and resilience . . . [Butler] touches on the strength of relationships among women—be they mothers, mentors, or friends." —*National Women's Review*

SORORITY
SISTERS

"Tajuana 'TJ' Butler's ripe novel *Sorority Sisters* . . . lifted the veil on life on line. . . . Not since Spike Lee's *School Daze* and the much-loved sitcom *A Different World* has the Black experience on campus been this intriguing and, at times, funny." —*Essence*

"Butler realistically captures the trials and tribulations of African-American college women. . . . Rarely has there been a depiction of African-American college life as vivid and accurate as *Sorority Sisters*."

—Lawrence C. Ross, Jr., author of *The Divine Nine:*
The History of African American Fraternities and Sororities

"A very engaging story about five African American college women struggling with campus life and the rigors of pledging. . . . Each woman matures to confront her insecurities through sheer determination to survive not only the pledging process but also the rite of passage between friends and the unique bonds of sorority sisterhood."   —*Booklist*

"*Sorority Sisters* keeps the pages turning."

—*Rap Pages*

"Butler's approach to the issues surrounding sororities and fraternities, sex and relationships, friendships and sisterhood, are all genuine and down to earth. *Sorority Sisters* is a relaxing read that offers a trip down memory lane for some and a heads-up for others."   —*Black Issues Book Review*

"Tajuana 'TJ' Butler scores big. . . . Serious subtexts involving STDs and loyalty never come across as preachy. Butler keeps her prose light and entertaining, making *Sorority Sisters* an enjoyable page-turner."   —*Honey*

"*Sorority Sisters* examines the issues facing women walking a tightrope between their teen years and adulthood. The author's vivid descriptions made me identify with the women's struggle and I felt their emotions keenly. And the fact that the author provided a peek into the pledge process of African-American sororities made the book even more tasty."   —Seventeen.com

PHOTO: WILLIAM COLE

ABOUT THE AUTHOR

TAJUANA "TJ" BUTLER is the author of the novel *Sorority Sisters* and the forthcoming *The Night Before Thirty*. She has published a collection of poetry, *Desires of a Woman*, and is a gifted public speaker. She lives in Los Angeles. For more information about Butler and her books, publicity tour, and other news, visit her website at www.tjbutler.com.

Also by Tajuana "TJ" Butler

The Night Before Thirty

Sorority Sisters

The Desires of a Woman: Poems Celebrating Womanhood

HAND-ME-DOWN
Heartache

A NOVEL

Tajuana "TJ" Butler

Villard • New York

2003 Villard Trade Paperback Edition

Copyright © 2001 by Tajuana "TJ" Butler
Reading group guide copyright © 2003 by Random House, Inc.
Excerpt from *The Night Before Thirty* copyright © 2003 by Tajuana "TJ" Butler

This work was originally published in hardcover by Villard Books, an imprint of The Random House Ballantine Publishing Group, a division of Random House, Inc., in 2001.

This book contains an excerpt from the forthcoming edition of *The Night Before Thirty* by Tajuana "TJ" Butler. This excerpt has been set for this edition only and may not reflect the final content of the forthcoming edition.

Library of Congress Cataloging-in-Publication Data
Butler, Tajuana.
    Hand-me-down heartache / Tajuana "TJ" Butler.
        p.   cm.
    ISBN 0-8129-6833-6
    1. Women college graduates—Fiction.   2. Mothers and daughters—Fiction.
3. Afro-American women—Fiction.   4. Atlanta (Ga.)—Fiction.   5. Young women—
Fiction.   I. Title.
    PS3552.U829 H36 2001
    813'.54—dc21   2001035772

Villard Books website address: www.villard.com
Printed in the United States of America

9 8 7 6 5 4 3

BOOK DESIGN BY MERCEDES EVERETT

To my mother, Linda, and my Mama Rachel

Acknowledgments

I am thankful to God, my heavenly Father, who carries me through the difficult seasons and balances my life with blessings and wonderful people.

Special thanks to my huge, beautiful family, the Macks and the Butlers, who have helped to shape my beliefs and values and continue to share their love and encouragement. I wished I could list you all individually, but you know who you are, and I love you all dearly. To my immediate, Raymond, Linda, Kim, Tracy, and my niece Jalyn. And my extended, Ellis, Lorenzo, and Phneshia.

To the "jewels," who are indispensable to my career and my sanity: to my editor, Melody Guy, you're simply incredible and I'm privileged to work with you; to my agent, Sarah Lazin, you're a godsend; to my accountant, Jackie Williams-Folks, you are invaluable; to my assistant and friend, Danielle Walker, thanks for helping me to become better organized; to my motivator, Mel Banks, Jr., you always know what to say to challenge my perspective.

Also, I'd like to express my respectful gratitude to the people who have touched my life in their own special way, be it great or small. You know why you're listed: Caren Handley, Keisha Tillman, Athena

Reese, Sandra Poindexter-Sowerby, Tracy Dennis, Felicia Radford, Stacia Carson, Lanetia Butler, Larry Muhammad, Jamilia Hunter, Maleeza Korley, Yolande Johnson, Dr. Mario E. Paz, Paula Balzer, Beth Pearson, Roger Patton, Tyler and Donna Reed, Collette Ramsey, Kenny Harris, Janice Jones, Jeffery Weaver, Kristin Vaughan, Lynn Shifflet, Wendy Nelson, Mike Austin, Ernestine Carrothers, Emma Rogers, Bro. Rasheed Ali, Bro. James Muhammad, Stephanie Thomas, Monice Mitchell, Ms. Lina Catalano, Sheri Smiley, Robert Zuckerman, Robert Abrams, Cordelle Rolle, Crystal Jackson, Elisa Freeman, Angela Stephens, Monique Johnson, Melissa Newton, Lawrence Ross, Elena Segatini-Bloom, Mitch Drone, Tony T. Fields, KJ in the Midday, BJ Murphy, Myron "Magic" Gigger, Justine Love, Vivian Carter, Rufus Beale, Maxx Myrick, Tobi Knight, Selma Dodson Tyler, Juan Shahid, Melissa Mitchell, Mark Mitchell, Charles Mitcheson, Tiffany Bradshaw, Nikki Bradley, Alfreda Vaughn.

The list is not by any means complete. I wish a special blessing to anyone whose name I failed to remember.

HAND-ME-DOWN
Heartache

Prologue

I met Ron at the wedding of my soror Chancey and her husband, Don. I just knew we were destined to share a heartfelt and meaningful moment or two. He was an usher and the best friend of Chancey's cousin David. I was a greeter. We were giving each other the eye as my soror Kendra and I directed guests toward him and David to be seated. Then when we stood on either side of the entrance to hold open the church doors for the wedding party, I was so into him that I nearly missed the opportunity to share a special moment with "my girls," the young ladies I had birthed into my sorority as their dean of pledges.

As the bridesmaids prepared to take their places next to their respective groomsmen, Ron and I locked eyes. Cajen interrupted our wordless flirtation with a gentle hug, then took her place in front of the line. She and the rest of the Phenomenal Five had grown so much over the last year. I can hardly believe that she was dean of our new line, or intake chair, as it's called now that hazing and pledging are illegal. Her talent for leadership made her the obvious choice. She had used the sorority to begin monthly Sisterly Awareness meetings, which had become very popular with young women on campus, who came to discuss such issues as dating, safe-sex, and self-love.

I had always had a thing for athletes, and Ron was wearing a championship ring. I noticed it as my glance went from Cajen to Miss Tiara, who squeezed my hand before taking her place. That girl is a mess and a natural-born comedian. We had really grown close over the last year, when I moved out of my apartment to save money and became residence director of her dorm. She became a residence assistant, and the young women in the dorm were lucky to have her. That girl is wise beyond her years and has street smarts. I'd learned a thing or two from Tiara myself, and I knew she was a shoo-in for the presidency of our sorority's chapter.

I caught Ron staring, but not at my eyes. I couldn't believe it; this brother was staring at my breasts. And he knew he was caught, because his eyes dropped down to his right foot, which suddenly began to tap. I wasn't sure if I felt flattered or turned off. I couldn't blame him for looking; my push-up bra made my breasts look kind of perky in this dress. I'd checked them out myself in the mirror before the wedding.

He looked up, tilted his head, and grinned shyly.

Okay, you're forgiven, I said with my smile.

"Malena, Malena, Malena. You're looking good, girl!" I whispered when we hugged. And it was true, though I knew she was a bit worried about the weight she'd gained since she and Ray stopped living together. She'd since moved in with her line sister, Stephanie, but between her breakup and her best friend Tammy getting married to Phil and moving to Germany because of his military assignment, it had been a tough year for her. But she had managed to get an internship last summer with the Terry Williams PR agency in New York, and they'd already offered her an entry-level position. She'd be moving to New York in the fall. The girl was no joke.

Then there was Stephanie, such a diva, with the grace of a swan. We kissed each other's cheek before she joined her counterpart in line. She too had had a tough year. Her biological mother was found dead in a crack house. Although she'd never talked much about her, the news had crushed her. Her line sisters, a few other members of the chapter, and I went to the funeral with her. Shortly afterward, she found out that she had a ten-year-old brother. She filed for custody, and her dealings with the court system prompted her to apply to law school. She had lined up a summer position as a legal secretary at a law firm in Savannah, where her brother was living with her adoptive parents. If all went well, she would begin law school in the fall, sharing custody of her brother with her parents, who would raise him until she graduated.

My attention moved back to Mr. All-American Eye Candy. He mouthed something to me, but I couldn't understand. The pianist began playing "The Wedding March," and Chancey walked by me and winked. She was a beautiful bride, seeing her in her elegant gown, I could hardly remember the shy, introverted freshman I met when she came to rush a year ago. Now she looked confident, and I knew she felt sure of her decision to get married before graduating. She would soon be moving to Chicago with Don, who'd been recruited into the NFL by the Bears. She planned to finish up her degree at Northwestern and embark on a new life as a player's wife, but she won't fit the stereotype; she's extremely intelligent and business-minded. I could see it: Don racking in the dollars, and Chancey investing them. By the time Don retires not only will they be set financially but so will their future generations. They would be a powerhouse couple and really work as a team. That's my idea of a good marriage.

After the beautiful and emotional ceremony, I rode over to the reception with Kendra, David, and Ron. Kendra and David were in the front seat and began talking to each other, giving me an opportunity to get to know Ron better. Our conversation was going well, which caused me to flirt a little more than usual. I batted my eyes and gently bit my bottom lip, just like Marilyn Monroe did in those old movies. Then I coyly moved closer to him and asked if he would save a dance for me at the reception.

I don't know if I had my Marilyn Monroe act down too well or what, but it was as if I'd flashed a green light and said, "Proceed to get your freak on ASAP." We were not on the same page. I wanted to flirt a little, but he wanted to mack a lot. He took the conversation to what he called "another level," and began whispering totally inappropriate things to me. He mentioned sexual positions he wanted to see me in that night and the things he wanted me to do with my tongue. Well, let's just say it turned me off. I couldn't believe my ears. I was so insulted.

"What did you say?" I snapped, and moved as far away from him as I could. "I know you don't think you're gonna talk to me like that, and I not have a problem with it."

Kendra and David abruptly stopped their conversation. Kendra turned around to see what was going on, and David looked at us through the rearview mirror.

"Nah, nah, baby," Ron said. "Just chill."

Kendra turned back around but peeked over her shoulder again to catch my eye and make sure everything was really all right. I calmed myself enough to let her know all was well. Then I looked back at Ron in disgust.

"My bad, baby," he said. "I'm only trying to have a good time. And I thought you were too, with the way you were coming on to me in the church."

"Yeah, I was flirting, but that doesn't give you permission to treat me like a ho."

"My bad. I just thought—"

"You thought wrong."

I didn't say another word. Neither did anyone else. Although the hotel where the reception was being held was not far from the church, it seemed like it took forever to get there. When we finally pulled up to the entrance, Ron jumped out of the car and walked over to two girls who were getting out of a car not too far from ours. He put his arm around one of them and fondly kissed her, as if trying to prove something to me. What, I'm not sure. Later I found out that she was his fiancée, poor girl. But I wasn't surprised. After all, all men cheat, right? It's the way of the world. And men sometimes forget to treat women with respect. Isn't it just their nature?

At the reception, even though I sat at a table with my sorors, I felt alone. I watched Don and Chancey, who were sitting in the middle of the dais. They seemed to be in love, at least for now. And I thought back to my flirting with Ron, whose fiancée probably trusted him. I wondered if relationships could work—I mean, really work. Was there the possibility of something worth holding on to, unlike the relationship of my parents, who live a lie every day, or my brother, who discards women as easily as he buys the latest CD to replace the one he loved the prior week?

Sitting there I had a feeling I wasn't quite prepared to go out into the real world. But I had no choice. Graduation was only a few weeks away. I wondered who I would become, and whether I would share my life with someone. And if so, what role would I play in that relationship? I certainly didn't want to be like my mother.

After the reception, I got a ride back to my car, which was parked at the church. I took the long way back to the dormitory, so I could have time to think. I had to be prepared for life after college, and I knew that if I thought hard enough, I would create the perfect plan. But nothing that I thought about that evening could prepare me for what was to come—for getting the opportunity to meet and understand the real me, and the side that I had been able to hide at college, where I appeared to have it all together. Nothing could do that but *life* itself.

The Reality of Life

One

$\mathcal{I}$ was back home in Atlanta and my best friend, Janelle, and I were sitting at the table, talking in my parent's kitchen. Janelle's dad came inside and stood by me. We spoke. Although I tried to hide it, I was fascinated by him and it showed. He asked me if I was looking for an older, stable man and said he would introduce me to one. I declined. Janelle's mom walked in, and she was well groomed and beautiful. My mom sat at the end of the table with her head lowered, her usual quiet self. Her eyes looked sad. I didn't want to say anything to her. I felt guilty because I wanted to distance myself from her, so I ignored her. Then my brother and Dad walked in. It took me awhile to acknowledge them because I was so captivated by Janelle's parents, their lives and their relationship. Suddenly it was time to go to sleep. Janelle and her family left. I stayed with my family. Our house was dark and gloomy, a mess. We had to sleep on the floor on worn mattresses. My dad was angry that we were around Janelle's family, especially her dad, earlier that day. I heard somebody scream. It was Mom. She was lying on her mattress, covered with blankets. She covered herself because she didn't want us to know she was hurt. I was afraid of what I would see if I pulled the covers off her, but I did it anyway. She seemed fine, but she was hiding something. I could tell. I told her that she shouldn't try to hide things from us, because we could handle the truth.

I woke up worried and afraid from yet another dream that I didn't understand. I tried to go back to sleep but spent the rest of the night tossing and turning.

.   .   .   .

I looked around the auditorium and spotted Janelle sitting in the audience. Seeing her made my smile even wider than it already was, if that was possible. I had attended her graduation the previous weekend at the University of Georgia. Seated next to her were my parents as well as my older and only brother, Brice, with his flavor of the week, Brianna. I heard my dad and Brice calling me by the nickname I had rejected as soon as I began high school: Ninu. I usually hated it when they called me that, but today I didn't mind it as much.

My stomach fluttered as the dean of Arts and Sciences called my name, Nina Yvette Lander. As I proudly walked down the aisle and onto the stage to receive my diploma, my family yelled, "We love you, Nina!" This ceremony was a pivotal time for me. I was happy to have those I loved there to share this step toward my new, adult life. Seeing their expressions of joy, I couldn't wait to join them in celebration.

After the ceremony my family, including Janelle, who was basically family because we had been friends since eighth grade, gathered around, congratulating me and taking pictures. It felt good to have them all together again. Tears welled up in my eyes. I hadn't expected that, but I welcomed them, wanting to hold this memory in my heart forever, in what I called my "good times place."

Mom was the first to hug me. "Congratulations, baby," she said.

"Thanks, Mom. Can you believe your youngest is now a college graduate?"

"I knew you had it in you," she replied. "I'm so proud."

Janelle and I hugged. "Look at you, growing up and everything!" she teased.

"Okay, grown woman, like we didn't just go through the same thing with you last weekend."

"I know, but it's different when you watch your best friend walk across the stage."

"Yeah, I know!"

Brice broke us up and hugged me with a back-breaking dip, muttering, "Stop hogging my sister, Janelle. Dang!" To me he said, "Congrats, bighead! Mom wasn't going to be satisfied until she had a college graduate in the family. Whew! Thanks for taking the pressure off."

"Just trying to pull my weight in the family," I replied.

"Hey, Nina, congratulations!" Brianna offered timidly.

"Why, thanks." I smiled, wondering how long it would be before Brice discarded her.

My dad had been standing back, giving everyone an opportunity to commend me, and then he took his turn. He grabbed my hands. "My Ninu is all grown up now!"

"This is true," I said. He looked at me with approving eyes. I felt proud of myself.

We hugged. "I'm so proud of you, even if it is a B.A. degree," he said.

"What's that supposed to mean?" I demanded.

"Just hoping for a master's soon," he replied.

"One step at a time, big fella," Brice said. He got between me and my dad and put his arms around our shoulders. "It's time to get this party started. Let's eat!"

We continued the celebration at my dad's favorite steak restaurant. I thought back to the days when I was a freshman in high school and Janelle would stay at my house over the weekend. We'd sleep in the basement after watching a Brat Pack movie on the big-screen TV and devouring pizza, popcorn, and Pepsi. Brice, then a senior, would be in the living room with some girl. He always managed to date "ladies," as he still refers to them, who had access to transportation and would sneak out and come over to the house.

It would be late at night and Mom would usually be upstairs sleeping. Back then my father always came in late and would catch Brice and his girlfriend "experimenting" on the sofa. He'd turn on the lights and ask the young lady, "Do your parents know where you are?"

That was Brice's cue to ask her to leave. After the "lady" left, nothing else was said about it. Even though he was caught red-handed, Brice and my dad would just sit up late and talk about sports.

I, on the other hand, wasn't allowed to date, except for my junior and senior proms. And even then I was not permitted to be in any room in the house alone with my date. I resented my dad's double standard. I always knew Brice was my father's favorite, so I became a sports fanatic just to have something to talk about with my dad.

Now I'd be returning home to Atlanta in the next two weeks, and my family would become a part of my daily life again. My mouth began to water at the thought of the wonderful Sunday dinners my mother would cook. And I knew I'd be shaking up the Atlanta party scene with Janelle, or at least that was what she had in mind. I would be close to my family again, and that made me feel happy, safe.

"So, Nina," my father broke into my daydream, "have you had any job leads since we talked to you last?"

I cringed. I had nothing to report to my father, who had just dished out four years' tuition. I had a journalism degree but no job offers. In college I was sports editor of the campus newspaper and hosted a sports talk show that I developed for the school's radio station, on which I interviewed our school's athletes about both sports- and campus-related issues. I had also interned with a few of the local radio and news stations in the city, but my inquiries about any journalism positions in Atlanta had gone unanswered. "Not yet," I responded.

"So, I guess you plan to live off me and your momma?" he joked, but I knew there was some concern behind his remark.

"No, Daddy. I have been sending out résumés. These things take time."

"Well, your brother's business is booming. Maybe you can work at the spa until something comes around for you."

"Negative," Brice interjected. "I can't have Ninu working for me. She'd know too much about my personal life." Realizing he had a part of his "personal life" at his side, he winced, then reached over and kissed Brianna on the cheek. "Not that I got anything to hide, baby."

"I wouldn't want to work for you anyway, Brice," I retorted.

"Daddy, I have some things lined up." I was exaggerating a little. I only had one lead: Janelle's boyfriend, Corey, and some of his associates had just purchased a small cable-TV station and were looking for talent to fill the time slots. I was confident about my abilities and looked forward to seeing how I could turn my love for sports and journalism into a career. Maybe this new station was a way, I hoped, but I wasn't particularly comfortable with that idea because I wanted to be at an established outlet. I just needed a chance to get my feet wet, but I think my dad expected me to graduate and somehow immediately be at the top of my game.

An uncomfortable silence came over the table.

Mom came to my rescue. "Didn't you enjoy the ceremony, Janelle?"

"Yes, ma'am, but it was much too long."

"Oh, I agree. Smitty almost fell asleep," she joked.

"Daddy!" I chided.

"Don't believe your momma. She's the one who was nodding off. I had to nudge her so that she'd be awake when they called your name." Laughter filled the table. I watched as mom laughed. I could see why my dad pursued her. My mom dressed conservatively and her gray hair was trimmed low and neatly kept. Even after having two children, she still managed to keep her shape, and her eyes looked alive when she smiled. But when she wasn't laughing, there were bags underneath those eyes and hurt behind them.

Dad's voice was low and husky and he threw back his head when he laughed. He looked good for his age, and he was always well groomed, with nicely trimmed salt-and-pepper hair and mustache. Although my dad was a blue-collar worker, his hands were always neatly manicured. He was tall and had once been slim, but now he had a round stomach from drinking beer and eating my mother's good cooking.

We finished our dinner without any further discussion of my career, thank goodness. I watched my mom and dad joking around. I had been worried about my mother after I left for college. She had seemed so depressed during my senior year in high school. Daddy was hardly ever around, and she was always making excuses for his absence. And when he was home, he was sometimes harsh with her. I never saw him raise his hand to her, but some of the things he said when he was angry at her made me ashamed to call him Dad.

Maybe now he'd appreciate my mom. From the way they got along that night, I hoped that Smitty Lander had decided to do the right thing and become a full-time husband to his wife.

.   .   .   .

After dinner Janelle and I went back to my dorm room and dressed for a party. It felt like old times as we shared the mirror and helped each other with hair and makeup.

"Nina, try this new lipstick," Janelle suggested. "It'll look good with your outfit."

"Okay." I took the tube from her and smiled. Some things never change about a person. Janelle was still high-maintenance, with manicured fingers and pedicured toes, an expensive hair weave, and designer clothes. She still offered me beauty tips and looked the same, only more mature. I had always envied her exquisite looks: her flawless dark brown complexion and the full, thick eyebrows that were always meticulously arched. She could have been a model; she was thin, five feet seven, and had high cheekbones and a beautiful face. She hated her thin lips, but had mastered lining them so they appeared fuller— which she was currently doing with patience and precision.

"By the time you finish lining your lips, I'll be all made up," I joked.

"You know beauty can't be rushed," she said.

That was my problem—I rushed the process. My daily beauty regime consisted of a light coat of mascara and lip gloss. But on special occasions, like tonight, I embellished more, and if I must say so, I do clean up pretty well. I am the girl next door: five feet five inches tall, with a nice smile and medium brown skin; my shoulder-length hair is generally loosely curled, and recently I've dyed it light brown with honey-blond highlights.

"So what do you think, do I need anything else?" I looked straight ahead into the mirror so Janelle could size me up.

"Nice. The lipstick looks good. Just let me line your eyebrows."

"Thanks," I replied. "I never can quite get them even." I sat on my bed while Janelle pulled out a liner and went to work on my brows. I began to mess with my hair.

"Be still, so I won't poke you in the eye," she fussed.

"I can't help it," I squealed. "I'm so excited. You're gonna like the sorors here. We're gonna have a good time!"

Once dressed, Janelle and I got into my car and headed off to one of the many graduation parties taking place that night. This one was off of the loop, which is the expressway to the city's suburbs; my sorors and other friends would be there. On the way we swapped pledging stories. It was funny that what had seemed so serious while we were on line was now absurd. We caught up on old times and reminisced about high school. We both agreed that although the time had gotten away from us, it seemed like yesterday.

"Do you remember our high school graduation party?" I asked.

"How can I forget? It was off the hook! They locked us in the gym until the next morning. The deejay was great, and we gambled all night and won a ton of fake money at the casino they set up."

"Oh, yeah, we had a ball. But the food was horrible."

"It sure was. Remember the watered-down punch? And stale potato chips?" She squinted and frowned at the memory.

"You convinced all your boyfriends to give you their fake money so you could buy a VCR to take with you to college because your parents wouldn't get you one."

"They weren't my boyfriends, but I do still have that VCR," she said. "You were so in love with Cedric! You two hugged and held hands all night long. It was disgusting."

"I was in love," I agreed. "He was my world back then."

"You always fall hard," Janelle said.

"I know."

Just then I saw a hubcap in the road but reacted too late. I drove right over it and my tire blew out. The car pulled to the left and I briefly lost control. Janelle started screaming, then I joined in. My life started to flash before my eyes. Damn, we were young and had just graduated from college, and now we might die. We shot past a car that swerved around, barely missing us. The driver laid on his horn. Another car veered around us before I was finally able to regain control of the wheel. I hit the brakes, stopping the car short of skidding into the soft left shoulder of the expressway.

Gripping the steering wheel with both hands, I looked around to confirm that we were still alive. I made eye contact with Janelle, who jumped out of the passenger-side door, leaned against the side of the car, and gave out a screech so loud that the sound moved down my spine. It was contagious. I jumped out of the car yelling, "Oh my God! Oh my God! OH! MY! GOD!" I'm not sure how long we screamed like hysterical lunatics, but eventually I regained my composure. I walked over to check the tire. It was shredded beyond repair. I shuddered, thinking about what could have happened.

"Okay, okay," I said, trying to calm myself. "Okay, we have to do something." I might as well have been talking to myself. Janelle was clutching her head and seemed to be in a trance. She must have been having an out-of-body experience.

"Janelle, snap out of it," I pleaded. "We have to think of a way to get this car to a service station."

She looked at me, but she still wasn't comprehending.

"Do you have your cell phone on you?" I asked.

"Huh?"

"Janelle, where's your phone?" I said more firmly.

"Oh, I left it at your place," she replied. Of course, I thought. What more could go wrong? "Where's yours?" she asked.

"I don't have one. So what now?" I knew I wasn't going to get an answer from her. I looked around. Cars zoomed by, blowing gusts of wind in their tracks, but nobody seemed to notice, or care, that we needed help.

I walked behind the car and looked down the road to see if there was an exit nearby that we might have passed. I didn't see anything, so I walked to the front of the car to check the road ahead and saw an exit that looked to be less than a mile up.

"I see an exit," I said, walking over to Janelle. "Come on, let's get back into the car." I nudged her.

"I'm not getting back in that thing," she said.

"Listen to me. We are near an exit. I promise you'll be all right."

"I can't move," she said.

"You have to, because if you don't, I'll have to leave you here," I threatened.

"Then you'll just have to leave me."

"Get in the car!" I yelled. Then I opened the passenger door and forced her inside.

I got back into the car and drove on the shoulder, riding the rim to the ramp. Janelle prayed the whole way. Silently, I did too. Thank God there was a gas station/convenience store right off the exit. I slowly turned the wheel, and the sound of the tire shifting from side to side on the rim was so loud that everyone noticed our not-so-grand entrance.

There were two guys in particular whose attention we caught. As we pulled in, one was walking out of the store and the other was pumping gas. Apparently the ride had brought Janelle back to life, because when I parked the car she instantly jumped out and gave her best damsel-in-distress look. I rolled my eyes, got out, and walked over to see how badly I'd damaged my rim.

Before I was able to analyze the situation a deep voice said from behind me, "It looks like you could use some help."

I turned around to see the guy who had walked out of the store.

"As a matter of fact we could," I replied. "I hit a loose hubcap back on the highway."

"Are you two okay?" he asked.

Janelle answered. "We're fine now that you're here." They exchanged glances and smiled. For Janelle, there's never a bad time to flirt.

"Do you know how to change a tire?" I asked.

"Yeah. Open the trunk, and I'll get the spare out," he said. We all walked to the trunk.

"Do you have a jack?" he asked.

"I'm not sure. As a matter of fact, this is my first flat tire."

He pulled back the mat, rummaged through the trunk, and lifted out the spare. Luckily he found a minijack.

Janelle and I watched as he jacked up the front right side of the car. There was a smoothness in his demeanor. He was an attractive guy, at least six feet tall, masculine, with full lips, dark, marblelike eyes, and coal black, neatly groomed hair. He seemed to have an easy-going personality. I wondered if he was in college, a local, or just visiting the city.

As his friend pulled their car next to ours, Janelle squatted beside him. "Thanks for helping us," she said. "So what's your name?"

"My name's Ian, and that's my friend Maurice pulling up," he said. Maurice got out of the car. He was tall, about six feet three, in top physical condition but not obviously attractive. He had a low-cut fade, and a mustache and goatee. I immediately felt like I knew him.

"Hey ladies," Maurice said. He first shook my hand, then Janelle's. "I see my boy is hooking y'all up."

"Yeah, he is," I said gratefully.

"So, where are you headed?" he asked.

"We were going out to a party."

"Yeah. We're on our way to a party ourselves. It's off the loop. Our boy just graduated, and we're in town to help him celebrate."

"Which party?" I asked.

"It's at the Hilton out in the burbs."

"That's where we're going," Janelle said.

"So, who's your friend?" I asked. "I just graduated myself."

"You might know him. His name is Tyrone Taylor, he played ball at—"

I interrupted excitedly, "TNT! I know him well. I've followed his college career since we were both freshmen. I must have interviewed him only a million times."

"Oh, so y'all know Ty." Maurice smiled.

"I'm not surprised. The Tyrone I know always has a way of meeting beautiful women," Ian said while tightening the lug nuts.

"This is a small world." Maurice seemed excited. "Yeah, we grew up with TNT. We all played together, but Ty went to college here, Ian went to Florida A&M, and I went to Georgetown."

That's when I made the connection. "I knew you looked familiar," I said. "I'm a fan. You're Maurice Crawford, a first-round draft hopeful."

Maurice stuck out his chest and flexed a bit. "That would be me."

"You had a ridiculously off-the-hook season," I commented.

"Yeah, but the team, man, we were not up to par."

"But you were great."

He seemed flattered. "Thank you."

"Finished!" Ian announced as he stood up and examined his hands, which were now covered with dirt and oil. "Are you closer to home or to the Hilton?" he asked.

"Probably the Hilton," I answered.

"Then I would advise you to drive there. But you'll need to catch a ride home after the party. This spare will only last for so many miles," he said, walking back over to examine his work, "so you might want to keep it parked there."

"Oh, no," Janelle groaned.

"I'll tell you what. We'll follow you to the party to make sure you get there safely. Then if you don't find a ride home with one of your friends, we could give you a lift. Your car will surely be safe at the hotel until Monday."

I wondered if maybe we should just drive back to my apartment. But how could I miss out on celebrating my graduation? I looked over to see what Janelle was thinking, but she and Ian had begun playing six degrees of separation, trying to figure out who she knew from Florida A&M. She appeared comfortable with the proposal.

"I'm sure we can get a ride home from somebody at the party," I said.

"And like my boy said, if not, we'll be glad to give you one," Maurice said, and touched my hand ever so slightly. It was a friendly touch.

Janelle and I got into my car, and Maurice and Ian trailed us to the party.

"So, what do you think?" Janelle asked me.

"I think the tire will hold up just fine," I answered.

"No, I mean about Maurice."

"He seems nice," I said.

"You are so full of it. You know you were checking him out."

"And?"

"You should get his number, you know, to stay in touch."

"I don't think he's my type of guy."

"What do you mean he's not your type of guy? He's exactly your type. You love athletes."

"Not necessarily to date."

"Most of your boyfriends have been athletes."

"Maybe I'm thinking about making a change," I said.

"That's cool too, but I don't see anything wrong with you making a new friend."

"What about Ian, you gonna get his number?" I wanted to move the focus from me.

"I thought about it. He is cute, but I promised Corey I'd be good this weekend," she said proudly.

"Since when did that stop you?" I joked.

"Since I fell in love."

"This Corey must be something special," I said.

"He is."

We made it safely and parked. They pulled in next to us. Then Maurice got out of the car and walked over and opened my door. He leaned into the car and said, "I'm sure this is going to be a pretty crowded party."

"Yeah, it will be," I said, getting out of the car. He backed away long enough for me to get to my feet.

"Well, I'd like to call you—if that's okay."

"Excuse me?" I said. Did he just want to make sure I got home okay, or did he want to talk?

"I'd actually like to get to know you better," he said shyly. "I think we might have a lot in common. I know you probably know a lot of people in there and will be celebrating."

I smiled. It was obvious he had been getting his approach together in the car on the way to the hotel. He continued, "And it would not be cool for me to chase you around the party, yelling in your ear over the loud music, trying to find out your favorite food or your future plans."

I noticed that Ian had made his way over to Janelle's side of the car. They probably planned this strategy. Didn't even give us a chance to run. But Maurice seemed nice enough, as did Ian. They did fix our flat and made sure we got to the party safely. Plus he had a certain charm going for him. I wanted to give him my number, but first I had to play a little hard-to-get. "I just met you. Why should I give you my number?"

He came back with a classic say-whatever-it-takes line, "You said earlier that you were a fan, which means you've seen me play, right?"

"Right."

"Well, I was hoping that maybe you could give me some pointers on my game." His smile grew even cuter.

I paused before I answered. He stopped smiling and said defensively, "If you don't want me to call, that's cool too." He backed away.

"Okay," I said teasingly. "You should call me because I do have a few pointers to give you that just might help you improve your jump shot."

Janelle and Ian stopped talking and looked over at Maurice, I guess to see how he would respond.

He laughed. "You're right, my jump shot does need improvement." He moved toward me again. "I look forward to learning any new techniques you may want to teach me."

Not another one. I couldn't believe this guy, especially after my run-in with Ron at Chancey's wedding. Why did I keep meeting the idiots who wanted too much too soon?

My reaction must have been obvious because he quickly clarified himself. "Ball-handling and shooting techniques, of course."

"Of course," I replied, realizing that maybe it was my mind and not his that was taking a swim in the gutter. I blushed and got my pen from my purse and gave him my number. Maurice had scored what I was sure would be the first of several phone numbers he'd get during the evening. Ian, on the other hand, didn't have a chance with Janelle. She thought he was attractive, but I knew she cared about Corey. Janelle had mastered the art of harmless flirting, and she always knew where to draw the line.

Two

By the time I moved back home, Maurice and I had developed a nice phone relationship. We continued speaking and I was really beginning to like him. He was a natural jokester and made me laugh. We talked a lot about sports. He told me that he wanted to be a teacher if he didn't get drafted into the NBA. I thought he'd be a great teacher. He had a gift for telling stories.

However, his enthusiasm for our conversations wasn't consistent. Some nights he'd call and we'd talk so long that one of us would nearly fall asleep. Other times I'd call and he'd seem to be in a bad mood and reluctant to talk. I'd apologize for calling at a bad time and tell him to call me later.

One particular time when I called and he was untalkative, I found the courage to confront him.

I said, "Maurice, if you don't want me to call you anymore, just tell me."

There was silence.

"Well, I guess I got my answer," I said angrily.

"No, Nina, wait," he said. "It's just been a bad week."

"You want to talk about it?"

"Not really."

"Oh!"

"I just don't want to bother you with my problems," he said.

"I wouldn't be bothered."

"Nina, I'm still in D.C. because I have one class to complete before I get my degree."

"And?"

"It's not going so well. But I'm determined to graduate. They're not keeping my degree. Then I'm feeling the stress of going back home to Detroit to wait for the draft. Home is depressing. I know I'm going to feel the pressure of taking care of my moms." I knew his parents were divorced.

"Is it that bad?" I asked.

"Let's talk about something else."

"Okay," I replied, not wanting to pry.

"Hey, why don't you come see me before I leave?" he asked. "You could spend my last weekend in town with me."

"I don't know," I said. I liked Maurice, but I wasn't sure I knew him well enough to spend a weekend with him.

"I'll be a perfect gentleman, I promise," he said. "Have you ever been to D.C.?"

"No."

"You'll love it here," he said. "I'll show you around and make sure you have a good time. I'm a great tour guide. Plus I could really use the company, Nina, and it will give us the opportunity to spend time together in person."

It sounded like a good idea. "Well, I need to think about it," I said.

"Okay."

After a few persuasive conversations with Maurice, I agreed to visit him, so we decided to split the cost of my plane ticket to D.C.

•   •   •   •

Getting to know Maurice diverted my mind from the tension between my parents. Smitty walked around like he was on top of the world. My mother, on the other hand, tiptoed through the house doing everything she could to please him, while he seemed more ungrateful than I ever remembered.

One night he came in late and yelled to my mother, who was already in bed, "Juanita, I'm hungry. What was for dinner?"

I hoped she'd yell back, "Look in the oven," or "I only cooked for Nina and me because you didn't have the decency to come home at dinnertime," but instead she dragged herself downstairs in her robe and prepared him a plate. It wouldn't have bothered me so much if he'd said something like "Thanks," or "Baby, you hooked up that chicken. It's too good." But he just stood in the kitchen looking helpless, watching my mother pull leftovers out of the oven.

She yawned, and he said sharply, "You act like it's a problem to fix your man's plate. Do we have a problem here?"

She answered calmly, "No, Smitty, there's no problem. I'm just tired, I've had a long day."

"From doing what?" he snapped. "It's not like you have a nine-to-five."

Mom quickly changed the subject. "How many rolls do you want?"

He answered, and with a blank expression on his face walked right by her down to the basement, where he turned on the television.

Momma brought him a warm plate of food, then busied herself close by to remain available until he called her to tell her he was finished. She took his plate away and washed it. He didn't want anything else, so she went back upstairs to their room.

I offered to wash dishes or help in the kitchen on several occasions, but she always insisted I go back to whatever it was I was doing. This picture was beginning to get underneath my skin. My mother went out of her way to please my dad. She prepared breakfast and dinner every day, and lunch on the weekends. Although she didn't work outside of the house—Daddy didn't allow it—she was always cleaning, fixing, and fussing over the most trivial things. And when she got tired, which seemed like often these days, she'd sit down to rest, but briefly, and every time she heard any little noise she'd jump up and pretend to be doing something, anything.

She seemed worried about being caught idle. I had just gotten off of the phone with Maurice that day, and I was feeling good. I'd had two callbacks on résumés I'd sent out, and Mom and I had a nice time together. Somehow we'd gotten to talking about the births of my brother and me. I listened intently as she exaggerated the fact that I was the tougher labor of the two and how she'd had no problem with Brice. She said he'd seemed eager to get here, but I wasn't sure whether I was ready. We were sitting at the kitchen table laughing and must not have heard the front door open and shut, because before we knew it my dad was standing there staring at my mother.

"Hey, Juanita," he said in a low tone. He looked angry.

My mom looked like a deer caught in headlights. She almost jumped out of her seat. Seeing me taking in the situation, she tried to appear calm. "Hey, Smitty, how was your day?" Her voice trembled. She looked as if she didn't know what to do with herself.

Daddy didn't say another word but continued to stare a hole through her. I started to feel frightened. What was going on here? What was he going to do? I wanted to distract him before he said something I didn't want to hear, so I jumped up, grabbed his hand, and said, "Hey Daddy! I noticed one of your new flowers has bloomed."

He snapped out of whatever it was that was coming over him. "Oh yeah?" He grinned and followed me out the back door and down the deck stairs to the yard, which was immaculately landscaped. My dad did all the gardening himself, working in the yard early every Saturday morning and Sunday right after church. Every since I could remember, my dad took pride in having the nicest lawn in the neighborhood.

As a child I always imagined that a giant had taken a huge house-shaped cookie cutter and formed each home in our neighborhood, then meticulously placed each one on its identical lot. They were all basically the same brick, two-story structures with slight differences in trim and color. But ours stood out because of the landscaping, as my dad proudly informed anyone who visited.

"Ninu, come see the begonias," he bragged. "See, Mr. Malone planted some after he saw how nice mine looked, but his don't look nearly as good as mine."

"They are beautiful," I said, attempting to appear interested. But I was thinking about my mother and how miserable she must be. She and my dad had been married for twenty-seven years. And although I don't remember most of my childhood—I know I was unhappy and blocked several events—I never remember her ever being ecstatic about life. She seemed to have a permanent frown, unless she was in public. Then she felt the need to prove to the world that she was happy. But anyone who was ever in her company for long could see through the façade.

How, I wondered, could my daddy, whom I cared so much for, be so gentle with his flowers, yet so monstrous toward my mother?

"Hey, Ninu, could you get my trimmers from the shed?" he asked. I wanted to say, Get your own trimmers, and why do you treat my mother so badly? But I opted to keep the peace and get them.

Daddy and I stayed in the yard for about an hour and a half. Although I could think of a ton of things I needed to do, I felt safe knowing that Momma was inside and I could watch his every move.

She finally called us in. "Dinner's ready," she said. "Smitty, Nina, come in and clean up so we can eat."

I began to make my way to the deck and noticed Daddy hadn't budged. "Daddy?"

"Huh?"

"Come on. It's time to eat."

"Okay," he said. And only after he did a once-over inspection of his work did he get off his knees and walk toward the house.

Here I was, a college graduate who had held several leadership positions and lived on my own for four years, feeling like a child again now that I was home. And not a happy one. That evening at the dinner table I found myself chattering on and on about whatever came to mind just to ease the tension. I thought back to childhood dinners, when Brice would talk nonstop with my dad about sports. I'd always thought that was their way of bonding, but now I had to wonder if Brice was doing then exactly what I was doing now: filling the miserable silence that had plagued our dinner table for many years.

After dinner my dad went into the basement to watch a movie on the big screen while I helped Mom in the kitchen. I insisted that she rest and let me clean up, but my mother had a way of not allowing anyone to do much of anything for her.

Neither of us mentioned the brief standoff earlier between her and Dad. I didn't know what to say, and I guess maybe she didn't either.

"You don't have to help me, Nina," she said while she washed the dishes. I dried.

"I know, but I want to. If I wasn't doing this, then what would I be doing?" I said. "I need to get a job, and soon."

She reached over the sink and grabbed my hand. She lowered her voice. "No matter what Smitty says, just promise me you'll hold out for something in your field."

I looked to see why she was whispering. Dad was nowhere around.

"I'm going to do my best."

"Promise me," she said.

"Okay." I was stunned, but glad that it meant that much to her.

She seemed satisfied and went back to washing dishes.

.   .   .   .

I had my own phone line at the house, even though my parents' phone hardly ever rang. My mother didn't spend idle time chatting with girlfriends. Although she was a member of a social group, the other women usually only made calls to the house to give her information or tell her about an event. I, on the other hand, enjoyed chatting with Janelle about every little thing.

She had called that evening with her news of the day. "Girl, guess which of our high school classmates just signed a record deal with Hip Hop Records?"

"Who?" I asked.

"Guess."

"Now you know I don't remember the names of our classmates."

"I know you've got the memory of a senile old lady, but you know this person."

"Male or female?" I asked, knowing Janelle wouldn't let me get out of playing this game.

"Male."

"So, did we graduate with him?"

"Yes. Give me your guess," she insisted.

"Eric Garrett," I said, referring to a guy who played drums in the band.

"Nowhere near," she said impatiently. "Guess again."

"Well, if I'm nowhere near, I'm never gonna get it right."

"Nah, you won't because I would have never guessed in a million years myself. I mean, this guy was a total nerd back then. Who knew he had rapping skills?"

"Why are you talking like I know who you're talking about?" I said, growing frustrated.

"Girl, Leonard Jones!"

"Who?" I searched my limited high school name-to-face memory bank. I couldn't place him.

"You know who I'm talking about. You're just not thinking."

"No, I don't think I do."

"I know your mother keeps your yearbook on the bookshelf in your room. Go get it," she instructed.

"I don't feel like getting up, Janelle. I had a long day."

"Doing what?" she demanded jokingly. "You don't have a job yet. Go get that yearbook."

"What's that supposed to mean?" I snapped.

"Lighten up, grown woman, I'm just kidding."

"My bad," I grumbled. "Hold on." I walked over to get the yearbook. I didn't mean to snap at her, but Dad had said the same thing to Mom earlier, and hearing it from Janelle just didn't sit well with me.

I thumbed through the yearbook until I got to the picture of Leonard Jones. I did remember him. At the end of every school year he would ask me to sign his yearbook to "Leo Jay." He always had a space reserved for me. I assumed he did that with everyone. We always spoke in passing, but I guess I never knew his real name.

"Oh, Leo Jay," I said. "I didn't know what his real name was. He wasn't a nerd. He was just quiet."

"Whatever. Anyway, he always had a crush on you."

"No he didn't."

"Yes he did. Why do you think you were always the first to sign his yearbook?"

"The first? So?"

"Do you think he ever even asked me to sign his yearbook?"

"I don't know," I replied.

"No, and I know I was one of the finest girls in that school."

"You're so silly," I said. We laughed.

"Anyway," she continued, "he now goes by LJ Love and he's been successful entertaining overseas and now has a rap album that's coming out in the U.S. I hear it's dope. And he's not looking so nerdy these days. I saw him on BET News tonight."

"Is that so?" I said dryly.

"Uh-huh. Maybe the two of you can rekindle that old flame now that he's getting ready to be a famous rapper."

"Girl, please."

"Just jokes," Janelle said. "So what's up, Anna Mae?" We both loved the movie about Tina Turner, *What's Love Got to Do with It*, and had seen and discussed it many times. We'd gotten "Anna Mae" from that, and used it as a term of endearment, acknowledging the strength we possessed as women.

"Girl, nothing," I said. Then I came clean. "I've been thinking about Maurice. I can't seem to get the brother off my mind."

"So what's up with your D.C. plans?" she asked.

"I leave next Friday. And I can't wait."

"Have you gone shopping yet?"

"I don't have the money."

"Girl, let's go tomorrow," she insisted.

"I said, I don't have the money."

"Ask your daddy for a loan."

"I'm changing the subject right now," I said. "So, what's going on at your job?"

"You're off the hook momentarily because I need to get this off my chest." Her voice deepened. "I am so tired of my job and my boss. Already. She gets on my last nerve."

"What did she do now?" I asked. But she continued as if she hadn't heard me.

"I signed up with a temp agency, and if they find me something making at least eleven dollars an hour, I'm walking out the door without a kiss, a good-bye, or a two-weeks' notice."

"Girl, what did she do?"

"The question is, what didn't she do?" Janelle began. "She still talks down to me as if I don't know my job. Then every time she's in a crunch because of her ignorance, she comes running to me to save her ass. And I always do."

"So what are you going to do?" I asked.

"I'm gonna keep looking for something else. But until then I gotta pay the bills."

"Well, do what you gotta do."

"So, are we going shopping or what?" Janelle asked.

"A new pair of shoes would be nice, but I'll have to sleep on it."

"Well, you do that, and call me in the morning."

"All right. Good night."

"Good night, Anna Mae."

Three

The day before I flew out to D.C., I let Janelle convince me to go shopping with her when she got off work. It was a good thing I did. We found some good bargains, and I was relieved to be out of the house. I hadn't ventured out much since I'd been home, with the exception of a few interviews and grocery shopping with Mom. The negative energy in that house lingered, nagging at me while I was out with Janelle. I definitely didn't want to expose her to my family's drama, so I attempted to make excuses about why she shouldn't come back to the house to help me pack.

"Why don't you want me to help you?" she asked as we sat and waited for the shoe salesman to return with our sizes. I was trying on a cute sandal that was on sale; Janelle had asked to try on an overpriced pump.

"Because," I offered weakly. Attempting to change the subject, I asked, "Where's Corey?"

"Well, he's working late tonight. He's putting a lot of time into building the new TV station."

"How's it coming?"

"They're progressing slowly, because Corey's being really careful.

He wants everything to work out," she said. "So when are you going to submit your proposal for your sports talk show?"

"I haven't decided on the format," I responded. "Plus there's so much I would need to put into it. I'm not sure if I'm ready for such a responsibility."

"Girl, you are ready. It's what you prepared for the whole time you were in college."

"You're right, but I was hoping to get more real-world and guided experience before I made a leap like this."

"Well, time waits for no man," Janelle said. "So, why don't you want me to go to your house?"

"It's my parents."

"What about them?"

"They're on the outs," I explained.

The salesman came back with our selections and fitted us one at a time.

"Those are sweet," Janelle said when I tried on the sandals. I stood up and checked them out in the mirror.

"They'll work. I think I'll get these."

Janelle walked over next to me to check out her pumps.

"What do you mean, on the outs? Nina, your parents haven't gotten along since I've known you. Or have you forgotten?"

"Was it that noticeable?"

"I guess you don't remember how you used to call me late at night and make me stay on the phone with you until Smitty stopped yelling at Juanita," Janelle said. She turned away from the mirror and gently grabbed my shoulder. "It's me you're talking to. I remember the first time you called me and told me he hit her. Why do you feel like you have to hide anything from me?"

"I guess I remember, vaguely." My main memory was that my mother always seemed unhappy and she and Dad's relationship was strained. I didn't remember there being fights. Once, when I was about twelve, I fixed a romantic candlelit dinner for them, but it was a disaster. I had the table laid out with our nice china and glassware. I called them into the dining room and forced them to sit down, then walked out. Feeling proud that my plan to cheer Mom up was working so well, I rushed back with a pitcher of Kool-Aid. Mom was crying. I froze. Dad shot me a disappointed look, then left the room. I ran to my mom, attempting to comfort her.

"Did I do something wrong?" I asked. It was not my intent to hurt her.

"No, baby, you didn't do anything wrong," she replied.

My dad was cold, but it was difficult for me to visualize him laying a hand on my mother, I thought to myself.

"I don't like these," Janelle said referring to her shoes. "Girl, with that bad memory of yours, you've probably blocked it all out. But that's what I'm here for. I'll be your memory. At least, I can take you back as far as the eighth grade. Anything earlier than that, you're on your own," she said, attempting to lighten the situation.

"So, did I cry, Janelle, when I called you?" I needed to know the details, but dredging up old stuff was painful.

"Sometimes. But mostly you wanted to talk about the future and what we would do after we graduated from college. You talked about being a sports announcer, and I talked about being a model."

"So, tell me again, why didn't you pursue modeling?" I asked as we walked back to our seats. I wanted to change the subject. This was becoming too uncomfortable for me. Something tugged at my memory, and whatever it was, I had a feeling it was best if it stayed forgotten for now.

"I don't know, Nina. I guess real life called and I just naturally followed the crowd and went to college. Do you think it's too late for me?"

"Well, maybe to be a supermodel, but you still got your looks. I'm sure you could do commercials. Or you could model for one of those malt liquor print ads." I wanted to make her laugh. "It will be you and Billy Dee posing in *Ebony* magazine."

"I'm not that old, Nina." She laughed.

"All right, then you and Snoop Doggy Dogg in *Vibe*."

"Just quit while you're ahead," she said. Then she got serious. "I'm not going home. I'd just be bored tonight. I'm helping you pack, okay?" She looked into my eyes, and I could see her concern.

"Okay, but don't think that I'm packing what you would pack if it were you going. You know I got to be me."

"That's a deal. But I am allowed to make suggestions, right?"

"We'll just have to see how it goes."

I was blessed to have Janelle as my friend, but I realized that I would eventually have to face my past. Having her in my corner helped to ease my fear.

．　　．　　．　　．

When Janelle and I got back to my house, Daddy's car wasn't there, but Brice's BMW was in the driveway. He popped over at the oddest times to check on Mom. Since I'd been home I noticed that he came by often, although he kept his visits brief. He still received mail at the house, so he'd stop by for that, then he'd go through the refrigerator and eat anything that could be quickly devoured.

"Oh, Brice is here," Janelle said. "I guess I will get some cheap thrills tonight."

"Please, if you and Brice ever get together, by any unlikely chance, please make sure I don't know about it."

"Oh, but you'd be the first to know," she teased. "But for tonight, I'm just going to enjoy watching your fine brother strut around the house."

Janelle had always had the biggest crush on Brice. I had to admit he was cute. He was six feet tall and always flashing his crooked smile. On some it would have seemed odd, but when he smiled he parted his lips just right, and when his mouth pulled to the left, it was downright sexy. He was a licensed barber, and he trimmed his hair daily. I think he stayed in the mirror longer than most women. Brice was comfortable with his manhood. He knew what his assets were and used them to their potential. At one point when he was younger he was extremely small for his age, but he started hitting the weights early on. He remained slim, but he was cut. By the time he was in high school, he walked around with his shirt open to show his six-pack whenever possible.

Janelle had once witnessed firsthand how ruthless Brice was with women when she was at our house and he had one of his girlfriends over. Two other women knocked at the door, and Janelle and I answered. They asked for Brice, so we let them in. We took them in to where he and his girlfriend were, and all hell broke loose. They busted him. The two women told the girl who was there with him that they'd found out that they were both dating Brice. And when they decided to confront him they had no idea she would be there too.

Brice's girlfriend cried the whole time. He didn't seem to care. He told them, "I never made a commitment to any of you, so please, get out of my house before you disturb my mother. All of you." He kicked everybody out, including the crying girlfriend.

Since then, Janelle chose to admire him from afar because she stood firm on her belief that she'd never put herself in the position of sharing a man. For Janelle, that would never do. Brice had asked me to hook him up with her several times, whenever he had a dry period. Thankfully, nothing had ever come of it.

I told Janelle it was naïve of her to think that she would ever be any man's only woman. She told me I was a settler. As far as I was concerned, Janelle lived in a fantasy world and I was a realist. We'd debated this issue on several occasions, with neither of us swaying from our beliefs. We always end with the understanding that Janelle would always see it her way and I would see it mine.

We got out of the car and walked into the house.

"Brice! Mom!" I called, then closed the door behind us.

"We're in here, Nina," Brice said. His voice came from the living room.

Janelle and I put our bags down in the foyer and walked inside. Brice and Mom sat on the edges of their seats. It was obvious that we'd interrupted a serious discussion. The television was off, which was unusual in our household. It was always a safe distraction from sharing more than was necessary.

"What's up?" I asked.

"Oh, nothing much. We're just talking," Mom said in a reassuring tone. "How are you, Janelle?" she asked, smiling.

"I'm fine, Mrs. Lander." I guess Janelle could tell there was more to the conversation than my mom let on because she usually talked to my mom like they were old chums.

"Hey bighead, I hear you're going to D.C. in the morning," Brice teased.

"Yep, that's right. I'm trying to get as far away from you as I can." I can't believe that as old as Brice was he still forced me to play this stupid sibling-rivalry game.

"Good, please go far away, because I could smell your stinky feet when you pulled up in the driveway."

"Oh, grow up!" I said. Sometimes he plays just too much.

"Brice," my mother scolded.

"My bad," Brice said with a laugh. "Do you need a ride to the airport?" This was his way of apologizing for going overboard.

"Nah, that's okay. Daddy's taking me."

"Okay, I'm just checking, because I wouldn't want my little sister to think I didn't care about her well-being," he said to me while leaning toward Mom and exaggerating the sincerity in his eyes.

"Oh, cut it out, Brice. Those puppy-dog eyes won't work on me," Mom said. "Maybe you should come over early in the morning and give your sister a ride." She swung to hit his arm, missing on purpose.

"Please don't torture me like that, Mom," he said.

"You two haven't spent much time together since you've been home," she said. "I think it's a good idea."

"You're right, Mom. Brice, be here at nine A.M., and don't be late."

"Wait a minute. How did this happen?" he protested. "Man!"

We all ignored Brice's plea to get out of picking me up in the morning. It was true, my brother and I needed to spend time together. Plus I was hoping to get some insight from him into the current status of Mom's and Dad's marriage.

"So, did you girls catch any good bargains at the mall?" my mom asked.

"Like mother, like daughter," Janelle said. "Nina wouldn't buy it unless it was on sale. But she's gonna be looking good on her trip, Mrs. Lander."

"Well, good. Nina, go get your bags and show me what you got."

"Okay, but are you sure everything is all right?" I asked.

"Girl, go get those bags," she demanded. "So Janelle, did you buy anything?"

I ran to the foyer and returned with my purchases. I showed Mom and Brice my finds while Janelle helped me explain how I would coordinate them with what I already owned. Brice interrupted, "What am I doing? I am not the least bit interested in this fashion show. I'm going to the kitchen to hook up some leftovers."

After we showed Mom everything she went into the kitchen to check on Brice, while Janelle and I went upstairs and began to piece outfits together and pack them.

Maybe whatever Mom and Brice had been talking about when Janelle and I walked in wasn't a big deal. But my mother is an extremely private woman, and she doesn't easily share her emotions, even with family members. Maybe that's why it was odd to see the exchange between her and Brice. Was I a little jealous? Yes, I always knew that Brice and Dad had a special relationship, but I felt good knowing that I was close to Mom. But while I had been away at college Mom and Brice seemed to have developed a special relationship of their own.

Four

The next morning, Friday, I walked downstairs with my bags to find Brice sitting at the kitchen table eating breakfast. I couldn't believe he was on time. As usual, Mom had prepared too much food and was going through her routine of forcing more on Brice, which he wasn't turning down.

"Hey, Nina, you ready for your big out-of-town date?" he asked.

"Sure am."

"Yeah, you have to go all the way to D.C. to get a date. That's sad," he teased.

"That aroma is calling my name," I said to my mother, ignoring him. I grabbed a plate and sat with him to enjoy a hearty breakfast.

We were discussing the sites in D.C. when Dad came down the stairs dressed for gardening. "Thanks, son, for taking Ninu to the airport. It'll allow me to get some work done in the garden before that hot sunlight peaks."

"No, problem, Dad," Brice replied.

Dad grabbed a couple of biscuits and piled on bacon, eggs, and fried potatoes, and put them on a plate and headed outside. Then he looked over his shoulder. "Juanita, could you bring me some orange juice and a glass of water and put them on the deck?" Without waiting for a response, he walked out the back door. Silence fell over the room. From the look on Brice's face, I could tell I wasn't the only one who hated it when Dad talked to Mom as if she were his servant. Mom appeared unfazed. She went to the cabinet and grabbed two glasses, carrying out her master's orders. My stomach turned. I lost my appetite.

"Well, I think we'd better be going," Brice said.

My sentiments exactly.

.   .   .   .

The ride to the airport was awkward at first. Neither of us wanted to discuss our parents' situation, so we just plain didn't talk. Brice popped in a CD to break up the silence. A classic Prince song from the *Purple Rain* soundtrack blared, putting a smile on both our faces.

When we were kids back in the eighties we'd blast that tape when we had to clean up the basement on Saturday mornings. When "I Would Die 4 U" and "Baby I'm a Star" came on, Brice would pretend to be Prince performing onstage and I would grab two pencils and become Sheila E, jamming on percussion. We were quite a duo.

The music seemed to ease the mood, and we headed from the suburbs to Highway 285. I wanted so badly to talk with him about what was going on, but I was afraid. Afraid that if I released my true feelings, something bad would happen, like Brice becoming angry with me, and I didn't want that. Although he was sometimes a pain, I loved my brother and I wanted to always feel that he was my ally.

The more I thought about it, and the closer we got to the airport, the more I became desperate to say something. The desperation outweighed my fear, and I blurted, "Why is our daddy such a jerk?"

The music was loud, and Brice either didn't hear me or was stalling for a response, because he lifted his eyebrows to acknowledge he knew I was talking to him, but he didn't say anything. I turned down the music. "Brice, why is Daddy so cruel to Momma?"

"What?" he asked.

"I mean, he acts like this tyrant and treats Mom like she's a slave or something. Brice, he doesn't love her."

"Then why would he stay with her all these years?" he asked.

"I don't know, Brice, but do you think what's going on in that house is love?" I yelled. I started to cry. Everything that I'd been holding in since I'd come home was rising to the surface. "And putting love aside, Dad doesn't even respect Mom. He treats her like shit! He cares more about that damn garden than he does her."

I looked out the window and saw the sign indicating that the airport exit was only a few miles away. Why did I even bother? What could possibly be said to make me feel better about the situation? But since I'd started, I decided to continue. "And furthermore, why haven't you ever said anything to Daddy?"

"So what am I supposed to do, beg him? Say, 'Daddy, please be nice to Mommy,' like some child?"

"No. Step to him like a man."

Brice took a deep breath. Apparently he didn't want to talk about it. "I've thought about saying something to him on several occasions. I even approached him once when I was younger, but it was useless. Dad told me to mind my own business, that I would understand better when I had my own wife."

"And you accepted that?"

"Nina, Dad is from the old school, when men just laid down the law and it was on the woman to accept it, and she stuck by him, come hell or high water. And that's what Mom is doing. They are both contributors to their situation."

"That doesn't make it right. She's miserable."

"No, it doesn't. But Nina . . ." His voice lowered, and an earnest look came over his face. "If she's that miserable, why doesn't she leave?"

Whoa, I thought. It had never occurred to me that Mom had the option to leave. I was so busy fixing in my mind what Daddy should or shouldn't do that I had never thought about her choices in the matter. I couldn't think of anything to say and fell deep into thought. Why did Mom choose to stay?

"What airline?" Brice asked.

"Delta," I responded.

We pulled up to Delta departures and got out of his car. He

walked around and got my bag out of the trunk. "Have a good time," he said, giving me a hug.

"I will."

"See you when you get back."

"Okay!" And that was that.

There was so much more we needed to discuss. His point of view gave me something to think about. I could tell that our parents' situation bothered Brice just as much as it did me, and that he was also obviously without a solution for them.

I watched Brice pull off. I am not going to let this affect my relationship with Maurice, I swore. I am going to have a good time this weekend.

Five

Thankfully the flight was uneventful. Maurice met me at the airport terminal, which was a good thing, because I had never flown into the Washington airport. It was strange seeing him again. Although we spoke often over the phone, I hadn't seen him since the flat-tire incident. I didn't know whether we'd hug, kiss, or say hi, and I think we were each sneaking glimpses to remember how the other actually looked.

In the midst of people bustling to get to and from flights, Maurice stood out like a superstar. For one thing, he was taller than average, but he also had such an overwhelming presence. It was as if a magnet was drawing me to him. He was dressed in dark slacks, and his loose shirt, which he wore untucked, followed the contour of his muscular chest as he walked toward me. I wanted to run to him and put my arms around him and lock tongues, but this wasn't television and I had to use some restraint, be a lady, and follow his lead.

"Welcome to D.C., Nina," he said, and removed my carry-on from my shoulder and put it on his. He plastered a grin on his face, but when I was finally able to look into his eyes, he seemed nervous.

"Thank you."

"So, would it be okay if I gave you a welcome hug?" he asked.

"A hug would work," I replied, and moved closer to him. He spread his arms wide and wrapped them around me. The vibe between us was a bit uncomfortable, yet familiar.

"That was nice," he said, almost whispering. Then he grabbed my hand and we walked toward the exit. He began going down the itinerary for the weekend. As we chatted about whatever came to mind, I started to relax, and I think he did too.

It was going to be an interesting weekend.

•　　•　　•　　•

My hunch proved to be right. Well, almost right. Maurice had planned to begin our weekend-long date with a trip to the Baltimore Harbor. We dropped my things off at his apartment, then headed to Baltimore before the Friday rush-hour traffic congested the highway.

The harbor was magnificent, and dotted by nice upscale shops and restaurants. As Maurice and I window-shopped at the boutiques, we shared dreams of future purchases.

He said, "When I get my first signing bonus, Maurice is gonna buy himself a phat crib, a Lincoln Navigator, and a big-screen television with surround sound."

"That's cool," I said.

"What about you, Nina?"

"I want to buy a big, beautiful home and work with a renowned interior designer to make it magnificent."

"That sounds dope," he said, and kissed me on my forehead. "Maybe one day we'll both see our dreams come true."

We ate an early dinner at the Cheesecake Factory there on the harbor. Maurice wasn't very talkative, so I carried the weight of the conversation, which was light and general.

After dinner we drove back to D.C., stopping near his apartment to rent a couple of videos.

Because he was moving soon, Maurice's apartment had only the basic necessities. He warned me that he'd packed up a lot of the place. There were boxes everywhere. The living room was bare except for a sofa and his entertainment system, which was still fully set up. There were no table or chairs in the kitchen, nor any cooking utensils, but he did have a microwave and a few frozen dinners. In his bedroom the bed was still standing, but there were only a few items of clothing in his closet.

Once he acquainted me with his place, Maurice appeared nervous again and didn't say much. He even seemed distant. I could tell that something was bothering him, but I had no idea what. Had I done something wrong?

"You can sleep in one of my T-shirts and a pair of my boxers if you want," he offered.

"Okay, that's cool," I said, although I had brought my own pajamas.

I went to the bathroom to change, while he changed in his bedroom. We met back in the living room to watch our movies.

"Do you want popcorn?"

"I guess," I answered.

"Okay." He got up and put a bag of popcorn into the microwave. Within minutes he was back.

Not much more was said, and I told myself that since he was ready to watch the movie he must feel that small talk wasn't necessary. But clearly the vibe between us had changed, and for no apparent reason. We lounged on his sofa, munched on popcorn, and watched the movies, an action flick, then a drama. We dozed off on the couch before the second movie ended.

Saturday moved along pretty quickly. First we borrowed bikes from his neighbors and rode on the George Washington Parkway. It reminded me of an old country road, with huge, beautiful trees lining either side. It was a sunny day with a nice breeze, and the parkway was a busy spot used by bikers as well as people Rollerblading, walking, and jogging. Maurice was still distant until midway through our outing. Nature must have fixed whatever he was dealing with, because the stress on his face eased a little and he started smiling more. Being surrounded by trees and near the water lifted my spirits as well.

I was impressed with his itinerary; there were no empty holes in our schedule. We cleaned up after bike riding, then went sightseeing. Maurice took me to all the touristy places. We went downtown to Pennsylvania Avenue and walked the full length of the White House. We also went to the Mall, where we viewed the Lincoln Memorial and the Reflecting Pool, the Capitol, the Washington Monument, the Smithsonian, and a few other museums. I was pleasantly surprised by his knowledge of the city. The tour showed me another side of him and I was reminded of why I liked him. He appeared confident and excited.

We drove around the city, and he pointed out important landmarks such as the Kennedy Center, and the Ford and Warner theaters. I felt myself falling for him, and I hoped to see more of this side of Maurice.

That evening we dined in Georgetown at Sequoia, a restaurant on the Washington Harbor. The ambiance was unbeatable: romantic white lights in the greenery, hardwood floors, and a full view of the harbor, all complemented by a live piano player filling the air with music. The cuisine was awesome. I ordered the lobster bisque and Maurice got the mahimahi. We sat at a table close to the water and watched the sailboats going by.

"Nina, I want to apologize if I've made you feel uncomfortable in any way," he said. "You know, I've got a lot going on right now. And it was bugging me all day yesterday."

"I could tell," I said.

"It got worse when you were in the bathroom changing last night. I checked my voice mail and there wasn't a call from my mother or my agent. I was expecting to hear from both of them."

"Why?" I asked.

"Well, it's personal. I mean, it's nothing worth going into. People think it's an easy life being an athlete. But there's a lot of pressure on me."

I remained silent and allowed him to vent.

"There's wondering what city I'll be moving to. Nina, you were able to choose where you wanted to live when you graduated. I don't have a choice in the matter."

I attempted my most understanding nod.

"Then there's my mother, who's already spending money that I haven't made yet," he complained. "Don't get me wrong, I love my moms, but her expectations of me are too high. What if I get hurt? Then it's over. I won't be able to fulfill her dreams or mine."

"Right."

"You know, I love playing pickup ball, but now I can't anymore. I have to protect my legs, which are my meal ticket."

"I wish I had your worries," I said to lighten the mood.

"See, I knew you wouldn't understand. Nobody understands what Maurice is going through. That's why I didn't say anything last night. I knew it would be a waste of time."

Wait a minute, I thought; when did this become my fault? How did I become the bad guy by trying to make him look at the situation from my eyes?

We completed our meal in silence. The lovely atmosphere of the restaurant was a waste. I couldn't even enjoy my dinner because I was replaying the conversation in my mind and trying to come up with ways to fix whatever had just happened.

My stomach churned. I knew I had to say something to turn the situation around. I liked Maurice, and I wanted us to be able to communicate. I wanted to try to build a relationship with him, and here we were, already butting heads. So I attempted to console him.

"Maurice, I know there is no way I can understand what you have to deal with, being an athlete and all. I'm sure that somebody like me couldn't even handle the pressure."

He looked at me for the first time since he'd fallen silent. I knew I had his attention, so I continued to stroke his ego. "You are one of the best basketball players around, and I know everything is going to work out for you, even though it may seem kind of tough right now."

"Like I said, you could never understand," he scoffed.

"Help me to understand," I offered.

He looked angry, then took a deep breath and began to go down a list of things that he thought were unfair in his life.

"My father beat up on my mother when I was a kid. He nearly

killed her the night he walked out of our lives forever. I hate him! If he ever tried to come back into my life, I would kill him, Nina!"

I was stunned. I could relate to the hurt he felt. But I couldn't dare share with Maurice my feelings about my own father. He was the one who needed to talk, not me. I was fine, I thought. At least I still loved my father; if I began to think that I could kill my dad, that's when I would need to talk to somebody.

"It's my responsibility to take care of my mother," Maurice continued. "She's seen the rough side of life. I want to help her retire so she'll never have to lift a finger again. Then I can be assured that if she cries at night, it wouldn't be because of money or bills."

"For sure," I said.

"It's like bad things always happen to me. My best friend was hit by a car and killed while jaywalking across a busy street when he was only twelve," he said, lowering his head. I thought for a moment that he was going to cry, but he took a deep breath and looked directly into my eyes. "Nina, can you imagine playing with your best friend one day, and the next he's gone forever?"

I gulped. My heart ached for him. "I'm sorry that you've experienced so much pain."

"I'm a man, Nina. Maurice has made it through it all," he said, assuring me and probably himself, "but sometimes it would be nice to have somebody to talk to instead of always having to go around being Maurice, the star athlete who has everything together. Well, sometimes things are not so together in Maurice's life!" He looked out the window.

"What about Ian and Tyrone?" I asked "Do you talk to them?"

He continued to look away. "Ian and Tyrone are my boys. They look up to me. How would I look trying to let them know about my problems?"

"Human," I replied. I could dish it, but I couldn't accept my advice for myself.

I felt for him, and I was flattered that he felt comfortable enough with me to share such intimate matters. I could relate to the helpless feeling of knowing that your father abused your mother. I could empathize with what it would feel like to have your best friend die at such a young age. And I was sure that the glitz and glamour of being an athlete were not all they were cracked up to be. But I couldn't imagine not having at least one person in my life who really knew me.

"Maurice, I respect you for sharing with me, and I understand why you were down last night. You have had some bad breaks." I began to slow my speech, hoping not to say the wrong thing. "You are a strong man, and I know that although life has dealt you a raw deal, you are special enough to break through those barriers."

He looked at me. "Do you really think so?" he asked.

"I know so," I said. "You're the man." I grabbed his hand.

Maurice seemed to feel better, but there was an aching inside of me that I didn't quite understand. I interpreted it to mean that we were bonding and that I was developing deep feelings for him.

After dinner we drove to Haines Point on the Potomac River. We walked to the railing bordering the water, leaned against it, and watched planes landing on a strip that was directly across the river. We didn't do much talking but were extremely intimate, hugging and kissing. He rubbed my shoulders and my arms and kissed my cheeks and my neck. It felt good to be close to him. The park was dark and other couples and groups were posted at comfortable distances along the water. Whether or not they could see our faces, we were publicly displaying our affection for each other. But I didn't care if anyone was watching. I felt a connection with Maurice and was caught up as our lips touched, then our tongues joined, and it felt perfect, right.

Maurice sat me on the rail, slid his hand up my dress, and slowly rubbed my thighs. Then he unzipped his pants. I was intoxicated by his presence, and excited by being in the open. He moved closer to me and slid his tongue into my mouth again. I welcomed it. While planes loudly landed across the river and people drove by, we were slowly exploring each other. I savored the moment and etched it in my mind. This was one memory that I definitely wanted to keep.

He wanted to go one step further, and although my body was screaming "Yes, yes," my mind wasn't cooperating. I just wasn't ready. I wanted to take it slow.

"Make love to me," he whispered in my ear.

"Here?"

"We're almost there. Let's go all the way."

"I'm not sure, Maurice."

"I want you," he said, nibbling on my ear.

As tempting as he was and as right as it felt, I responded, "I can't. Not yet."

"Okay," he said abruptly, then zipped his pants. "No means no, right?"

"Yeah," I replied timidly.

He moved away from the railing and paced back and forth in the grass, obviously cooling off.

"Come here," I said.

He huffed.

"Come here."

He slowly walked back over to me. Then I began to kiss his cheek, slowly and softly, then his neck.

"See, you're getting started again." He smiled and kissed me back. I thought all was well until he abruptly stopped. "Nina, don't give me mixed signals."

I took heed and pulled away, turning to watch an airplane land. He watched too.

"You ready to go?" he eventually asked.

"Yeah," I replied. I was disappointed. I wanted to please him and I wanted to be pleased, but the thought of having sex with Maurice brought back that strange aching feeling in my stomach. I didn't understand it, but I wanted to know what it meant. I knew that I liked Maurice and wanted to continue seeing him. But after the ups and downs of the weekend, sex that night would have been too confusing.

He helped me off the rail, and I took one more glance over my shoulder at the moonlit water before we walked to the car. We shared an uneasy silence as we drove away from the park.

I reached across and put my hand over his. He didn't look at me or say anything, but he didn't ask me to remove my hand, so I knew all was well between us.

I assumed we were going back to his place.

"There's a house party going on near my apartment," he said. "Let's stop."

"Okay," I agreed. I wasn't ready to go back to his apartment and a party sounded like a good distraction.

There were probably more people crowded inside the apartment than the fire code allowed, but nobody seemed to mind. People still coupled up and danced. It was an upbeat, laid-back atmosphere, and Maurice introduced me to several of his friends. A few of his old teammates were there. They were all pretty friendly. Maurice seemed proud to have me meet everyone, and he held my hand the entire time. Everyone seemed to like Maurice, but he didn't seem especially close to anyone in particular.

We found a corner and Maurice began giving me the lowdown on just about every person in the room. I was dumbstruck by how perceptive and aware he was of other people's shortcomings.

The music had a good beat, and I was moving and snapping my fingers. "You wanna dance?" I asked.

He didn't, but he did want to be close to me, so we spent the rest of the evening kissing and touching there in the corner. I enjoyed seeing him excited, so I went along with his program. When we finally left the party, I was feeling a jones for Maurice. We went back to his apartment and had sex like there was no tomorrow.

I left D.C. in lust.

What Time Reveals

Six

"*F*uck you!" I yelled.

He stared at me as if he couldn't believe such words were coming from my mouth. And because we were in the upstairs hallway of his teammate's home, he probably felt he had to redeem himself in case the other basketball players or partygoers heard him being told where to get off. So after recovering, he screamed back, "Fuck me? Naw, fuck you!"

We were both out of control, emotional wrecks.

With nothing else left to be said, he stormed toward the bedroom door, flung it open, walked in, and slammed it behind him. I stood there alone, feeling empty, defeated.

We had been together for about five and a half months, and the basketball season was just beginning. It was supposed to be an exciting time for us both. But it wasn't. We should have been enjoying the party and then planning to go to his place afterward to whisper passionately in each other's ears and make wild love. But instead we were yelling and screaming and going our separate ways.

Maurice had been drafted into the Miami Heat. I had visited him in Miami on a few occasions and met some of his new teammates and their girlfriends. I clicked with one in particular, Cindy High, who was an anchorwoman for the local news station. I knew I could learn a lot from her and was fascinated by her drive and determination to succeed, so we had begun corresponding by e-mail.

I had gotten a position with Turner Broadcasting Network through a temporary agency. It wasn't what I wanted, but it gave me extra spending money and allowed me to see my savings account grow ever so slightly.

Her fiancé, Junie Peeh, who had been with the team for several years, was throwing a party, and she had invited me. I thought it would be a good idea. Maurice had mentioned the party a few times but didn't invite me. I could surprise him and add spice to our relationship, which was beginning to fizzle. Our communication when we were apart was lacking, but every time we were together, he clung to me. He always hated for me to leave.

After work on Friday I flew into Miami for the weekend and took a cab to Cindy's luxury high-rise condo on Miami Beach. We got dressed for the evening. Cindy put on a gorgeous designer evening outfit, a matching halter and pants. Janelle and I had gone shopping the prior weekend and I'd bought a hot red Armani knockoff along with tall, red Charles David sandals to accessorize.

"I am definitely making a statement," I said. "I can't wait to surprise Maurice." I looked in the mirror and admired how the dress and the highlights in my hair complemented my skin color.

"You're gonna knock him out with that dress," Cindy agreed.

"That's the plan!" I winked.

A limousine picked us up and chauffeured us to her boyfriend's house out in Coconut Grove. By the time we got there, the party was in full swing. As we approached the house it seemed to vibrate with music and conversation, and I got nervous. Maybe Maurice wasn't the type who liked surprises. I could feel tension growing in my right shoulder and reached to massage some of it out.

When we walked through the door I was immediately overwhelmed by the number of people I saw. I overheard conversations about subjects that ranged from sports to who's-who to finance. There were even more people in the backyard, where two large tents were set up and a deejay was spinning records.

"I see my man," Cindy said. "Come on."

Cindy found Junie inside. "Hey, handsome," she said, and kissed him on the cheek. "You remember Nina, right?"

"Oh, yeah," Junie said. "Hey, Nina, thanks for coming."

"Is Maurice here?" Nina asked.

"I don't know. He may be," Junie said.

"Relax, Nina. You're gonna see him soon enough!" Cindy said. "So, honey, do you need me to help with anything?" she asked.

"No, baby, everything seems to be under control."

"Okay. I'm going to show Nina around outside."

"Sounds good, but don't forget to get a wristband to get back inside. The security won't know you're my baby and they might not let you back in."

"All right," she said, and they kissed again.

"I just love him," she said to me.

"He seems nice," I replied, but I was preoccupied with trying to find my own man.

We picked up wristbands and went outside. The deejay was spinning the hottest hip-hop and Florida dance music. The dance floor was jam packed and busting at the seams.

In one of the tents was a fabulous array of hors d'oeuvres and seafood including shrimp, crab legs, and oysters on the halfshell. The wet bar was fully stocked, and there was even a cigar roller. Inside the second tent were black leather sofas and a big-screen TV turned to some sports channel. People were lounging on the sofas, standing in line to get food, conversing in lawn chairs placed around the grounds. There were basketball, football, and baseball players, actors and actresses, and musicians. Cindy introduced me to so many people with such a wide variety of job titles and professions that I almost couldn't keep up. This party was overwhelming.

Some people were feeling the party a little too much, but the overall atmosphere was quite glamorous, with bottles of Cristal and Dom Pérignon being popped open all over the place. Cindy informed me that a few of the guests who were singers were going to perform later. This was a new experience for me, and I saw a bit of everything—except who I really came there to see: Maurice. Where was he?

We ran into a couple of his teammates, and Cindy asked them about Maurice.

"Hey, Mitch, have you seen Maurice?" she asked one player, who probably had had too much to drink.

"Maurice who?" Mitch asked.

"Maurice Crawford," Cindy and I said together.

"Oh, okay! Do you know where he is?" he asked, scratching his head.

"No, that's why we're asking you," Cindy replied.

"He's here. I'm sure of it. Look around. The entire NBA is here." Cindy looked at me. "He's too drunk to know where he is."

"I hope he doesn't hurt himself," I said as he walked past us and into a tent where he took a seat on one of the sofas.

"Rodney, where's Maurice?"

"I think he's inside," Rodney said uncertainly.

"Thanks!" Cindy said. "Let's go inside. If we don't see him downstairs, we'll try upstairs."

"Okay," I said, discouraged. "But if I would've known we were gonna be doing this much walking, I would have worn flats. These shoes were not made for trekking."

"I know what you mean."

"What if he's not here?"

"Relax. I'm sure he's here somewhere. Maybe he had to make a call or something and needed a quiet place. You want to get a drink before we go in?"

"Yeah, that's cool."

We grabbed glasses of champagne and went inside, but Maurice wasn't in the game room, the home theater, or the living room. I could tell I was wearing Cindy down. "Why don't you spend some time with Junie?" I said. "I'll keep looking."

She didn't hesitate. "Okay, but don't forget to check upstairs. Oh, and come find us after you find him."

"All right." I nodded and continued my search. I was beginning to think that either he hadn't arrived or he wasn't coming. The rooms upstairs were as elegant as the rest of the house. Most of them were empty, and one was locked. I walked by it and checked the other rooms. Nothing.

I had a feeling that something wasn't right, so I got up the courage to knock on the locked door. I had hit the jackpot. To my relief Maurice opened the door, saying, "Hey, what took you so long?" When he saw me, he was shocked.

"Maurice?"

"Nina, what are you doing here?"

"Well, I wanted to surprise you!" I replied, excited to see him. "So, are you gonna let me in?"

Maurice stepped in front of the door, blocking the entrance. He looked at his watch and said, "Why don't you let me finish up in here, and I'll meet you downstairs."

"I'm fine. I've seen more of this man's home than I wanted to, and my feet need a break. I'll just wait for you." I pushed him aside and walked into the room. I stopped dead in my tracks because lying on the bed, wearing nothing but the shortest shorts I've ever seen, were two bimbos, one white and one black. I don't think I even saw their faces—they were all breasts and legs.

They looked at me, gave me cheesy grins, and said, "Hi!" in unison. They didn't even have enough sense to cover up.

I looked at Maurice, hoping for an explanation, an apology, something. But the jerk had the nerve to say, "Nina, can I talk to you in the hall?"

"What do you mean can you talk to me in the hall? If you want to talk, it's gonna happen right here in this room."

He grabbed me by my arm and pulled me out into the hall as if I was the one who'd been caught behaving inappropriately.

"Why are you pulling my arm, like I've done something wrong?" I asked him.

"Why don't you go downstairs and give me a minute and we can discuss this later?" he said, sounding annoyed.

"Oh, so you're asking me to leave?" I couldn't believe him.

"I don't know why you're causing a scene. Those are just some girls that I went to college with. They came down for the party. Why is that such a big deal?"

"Maurice, they're naked," I yelled.

"Ah . . . well . . . I didn't ask them to take their shirts off."

"You didn't stop them either."

"They're professional strippers, Nina, paying their way through school."

I was beginning to think that maybe I needed to take anger-control classes, because I swear I wanted to swing and punch him in his ugly face.

"Whatever, Maurice."

Did he think I was that big an idiot? Did he think I'd say okay, you go back and finish reminiscing with your old college chums, and I'll wait for you to join me at the party, my dear?

I calmly explained, "See, I think you've mistaken me for your pet chow, who comes and goes at your command, eager to accept your love whenever you choose to give it." I went from crossing my arms to pointing in his face to putting my hands on my hips to get his full attention. "But in case you're confused, let me clear your mind. I am a woman, not a pet, and I expect to be treated with respect. And I've come to realize over the past five months that you don't have the brain capacity to understand the concept of respecting a woman, therefore, I don't see any reason to allow you the privilege of knowing me anymore." I turned away from him and began walking toward the stairs.

I knew he hated it when I talked calmly during an argument and said more than he felt was necessary. And I truly believed he wanted me to cry or make a scene, because instead of turning away, he said, "So it's just that easy for you to walk away from this relationship."

He couldn't see my face, but I was grinning from ear to ear. I wanted him to stop me. I needed him to continue the conversation, because that meant that he cared. I didn't want to think about what was going on in that room, but at least he still cared about me.

I wiped the smile away and replaced it with a stern façade, then turned to face him. "Yeah, it is that easy for me to walk away, just like it's so easy for you to screw anything with big breasts and a short skirt."

"You are so immature," he said.

Me, immature? He was the one who couldn't handle getting caught with his pants down. Forget dignity. Something in me broke. And that's when the four-letter word raced out of my mouth. "Fuck you!"

"Fuck me? Naw, fuck you!"

I didn't turn around, just continued down the steps. I pushed through the people in the house to the front yard. Cindy followed me out the front door. "Are you okay, Nina?" she asked.

"I'm okay," I said, trying to hold in my tears. I didn't want to spoil her evening just because mine was ruined. "I just want to go back to your place, if you don't mind."

"Okay," she said.

"But you stay here," I insisted. "I'll just have one of the drivers take me back."

She grabbed my hands and looked into my eyes. "Are you sure?" she asked.

"Listen, you have a good time. I don't want to spoil your fun, and after what I just saw, I need some time to myself."

"What happened?"

Thinking about the scene upstairs brought tears to my eyes. "I'll tell you about it tomorrow," I said.

"Hold on. Let me get my keys for you." She walked inside. I had an awful time trying to hold back my tears. And while I stood on the front porch watching people come and go, I realized that Maurice didn't even bother to come downstairs and see if I was okay. My heart felt like it was being torn apart, and Cindy wasn't moving fast enough.

What had I done to make him want to be with other women? I went over in my mind the first three months with Maurice. Back then we were inseparable. We took turns calling each other every night when he was staying with his mother. Over the phone we realized that we had a lot in common. He was impressed with my knowledge of sports, and I with his sincere eagerness to achieve. Maurice had even come to Atlanta to visit with me a few times before he was drafted and moved to Miami. We'd stayed at my brother's house and sometimes double-dated with Brice and Brianna or Janelle and Corey. My family seemed to like him and welcomed him, which made me adore him even more.

Once when we went out dancing with Brice and Brianna at the Atlanta Dance Factory, I caught Maurice in some hoochie's face, getting her number. Her clothes were too tight, and she showed more cleavage than necessary. I lost my cool. Not wanting to make a scene, I waited until he got her number and walked away before confronting him.

"Maurice," I said. "I saw you taking that girl's number. So you think you can pick up some girl in front of my face?"

"Nina, that wasn't nothing."

"Well, if it wasn't anything, then give me the number so I can tear it up," I demanded, reaching in his pants pocket to get the slip of paper.

Maurice grabbed my wrist and squeezed it tight.

"You're hurting me," I said firmly.

"Good, because as long as you are walking on two feet, don't ever tell me what I'm going to do," he said. His eyes were hard and cold. "There will always be women who are going to give me their number, but that doesn't matter. I usually throw them away anyway. What matters is what we have, but if you keep acting like this, we won't have nothing." He flung my wrist away, then said he was going to the men's room.

My face was on fire. I was both embarrassed and frightened, I was fighting tears. While he had hurt my wrist, I didn't consider what he had done to me abusive. Yet there was something in his eyes and his tone that put the fear of God in me. I knew at that point that there were certain lines I couldn't cross with this man.

Now here we were, months later, and I was still love-struck. Despite his likely infidelity, and his temper, I still saw the good in him. After all, he had offered to add money to my savings account, and after I had declined, he called Brice and did it anyway. He had wanted to fly me to meet him in cities that he would be playing in that I had never visited.

I began to feel guilty and embarrassed—I had provoked him. I'd crossed the line, and things would never be the same between us. I had to move, so I slowly walked toward the limo. Cindy caught up with me. She gave me her key and directions to the driver, then she hugged me good-bye.

"Do you need anything?" she asked.

"I'll be fine." I attempted a smile.

The limo door didn't close fast enough, because as soon as I sat down, the harder it became to fight the tears. As the car drove away from the house I felt safe enough to release my emotions. Tears flowed down my cheeks, and I fell on the seat crying all the way to Cindy's apartment. As strong as I tried to be, the sad reality was that when he did try to come back, and I knew he would, I would take him back. All men cheat. My daddy had cheated on my mother since I could remember, and my brother never had just one girlfriend at a time.

I don't even think I was angry that Maurice cheated. But damn, why did I have to catch him with two groupies who were ready to get their groove on with no strings attached? And why did men have to be so insensitive? I mean, couldn't he have been more discreet? And why did I choose that particular party to surprise him, only to have thrown in my face what I already knew was true: Maurice was a typical male.

Seven

$\mathcal{I}$ was able to tuck the past weekend's incident deep in my heart and not think about it because I had other pressing details to tend to. The kind of things that you have to deal with even when your heart isn't into it. For one, I had to make my new loft livable. I hadn't expected to move into my own place so soon. At first staying with my parents had made sense, especially when I thought about the money I could save if I lived with them for at least a year—enough for a sizable down payment on a house, condo, or townhouse, any kind of home, as long as it had my name on it. Ownership has always been important to me. It's something my dad had stressed since he and my mom bought their first home.

They bought our house when Dad got a job with a new factory. It paid well, and my dad worked hard and, as he always said, "smart," and eventually became a manager. He worked there for twenty years. The company had a generous investment program for its employees, and my dad got in on the initial offering. It turned out to be a wise decision, and as his shares increased, he took an investment course and over time established a diversified portfolio.

Brice had sought ownership immediately after high school. Although my mother had insisted he attend a four-year college, he'd gotten Dad to ally with him and went to barberschool, then convinced Dad to invest money so he could open his own barbershop. Dad was 100 percent behind Brice being his own boss. That was six years ago, and since then the barbershop had flourished into a full-service day spa and unisex salon. When Brice offered to pay Dad back for his initial investment, Dad told him the money was a gift, since he did so well with it. So my brother used it as a hefty down payment on a beautiful two-story home in the Southland neighborhood in Stone Mountain.

And there I was, a college graduate, working a temp job at CNN, barely making twenty thousand a year, and living in downtown Atlanta in a loft I was sacrificing to afford. I knew that my dad would never invest money in my purchasing a home, at least until I had a job that he would consider satisfactory.

My plan to save for a purchase was stymied because I couldn't deal with hearing my mother cry herself to sleep, and seeing my father coming in at all times of the night and claiming it was business-related. I hated the silence between them during breakfast the next morning. The only words that he felt he needed to speak were commands and demands of his servant/wife.

There was never any arguing; my mother would do whatever it took to keep him calm, but the tension in the household was thick. I was beginning to hate my dad for disrespecting my mother and our family, and hate my mom for allowing herself to be disrespected. When my own emotions concerning their relationship began to add to the situation, I knew it was time to go.

I lasted in my parents' house for six months, just long enough to get employment and find a new place to call home. My search for a place took so long because I wanted to live downtown, but I didn't have high-rise capital. I have always had a thing for scenery and ambiance, and I wasn't going to accept any hole-in-the-wall apartment just to live downtown.

I was tending to details, details, details: hanging pictures and arranging what little furniture I owned: a bed, a sofa, a desk, and a few other odd pieces given to me by my mother. I was trying to figure out how I could have an office area and a living area side-by-side, yet have the room flow according to proper feng shui, when the bell sounded. Security is an issue for me, probably because I'd been having wild dreams since I graduated from college, so it was important that my building have an intercom system. I pushed the button and said, "May I help you?"

"It's Maurice, Nina. I have a housewarming gift for you."

My heart raced. I was excited, angry, turned on and off all at the same time. I knew he'd come back, but I hadn't expected it to be so soon. I knew he had a game in town the next day, but how had he found my new place?

"Why should I let you in?" I asked.

"Don't you want your gift?" He sounded excited, upbeat.

I did, but not the one he had for me. My gift was him coming back, just like I knew he would. But I had to play hard-to-get, so I paused for a few seconds, then I buzzed him in. I became increasingly excited as I heard him ascending the hardwood steps that led to my apartment. He knocked. I took a deep breath and tried to appear cool and unfazed by his being there.

I opened the door, and there stood a grinning Maurice, holding a huge painting in his hands. It was an original, a sorority piece by WAK, matted and framed. I was surprised because Maurice had never seemed to care much for sororities or fraternities, and especially their paraphernalia.

"Thank you," I said. "It's a nice piece." I wanted to seem congenial but not overly appreciative. "So, how did you find out where I live?" I asked as I took the painting and leaned it against the wall nearest the door.

"Oh, I stopped by and got a trim from your brother, and he gave me your address and new number."

"I told him not to give my new info to anyone."

"Yeah, he told me, but I bribed him with tickets to the game tomorrow night."

I was angry at Brice for betraying me, especially for tickets to a game, but glad that Maurice had made an effort to find me.

"Are you gonna be there?" he asked.

"Don't have tickets."

"Well, you do now. Two. Third row from the court. They'll be at will-call."

"Well, I guess I'll be there." I smiled.

"Nina, I missed you," he said, then walked toward me and carefully put his arms around me. Initially I stiffened in his embrace. But so much had happened since my graduation six months ago. I felt lonely, tired of trying to be strong and independent. I desperately needed to feel a moment of peace, and Maurice's embrace gave me that. I held him tight. I felt a temporary release from the stresses I'd been faced with: breaking up with him, moving into my own place before I was ready, and working a position for which I was overqualified.

I didn't want to let him go. He cupped my chin in his hand and wrapped his tongue around mine. When we finally broke apart he stared intensely into my eyes. "I need you," he said. "I mean it, Nina. I missed you, and I need to know you're in my corner."

I remained silent. He continued. "And I apologize for hurting you, when I knew you were only trying to make me happy."

That was all I needed to hear—his apology for disrespecting me. My dad would never have apologized for treating my mother badly. I had to forgive Maurice, because he was genuine in recognizing he'd been wrong.

"Are we cool?" he asked, pulling me into him. I timidly nodded. "Are we?" he asked again.

"Yeah, we're cool."

"Okay," he said, then began to kiss my forehead and my cheeks, my neck and my ears. The next thing I knew we were on the floor, tearing off each other's clothes in a frenzy. There wasn't much foreplay, other than the making up itself—it was an unspoken understanding. Maurice grabbed a condom from his pants but couldn't get it out of the wrapper fast enough, so I took it from him, tore it open, and put it on for him. I loved that act of endearment, and he seemed to also.

We were both panting loudly until he penetrated me. Tears began rolling down my face; I knew this moment wouldn't last forever, and as much as I wanted to keep him there with me, suspended in time, I knew I couldn't. He wiped the tears from my eyes and said, "Everything between us is going to be just fine." I relaxed, and we calmed our pace.

I savored every touch, every kiss, every thrust. I didn't want to ever have an orgasm because it would end the only act that I shared with him that made me feel like our relationship was on an equal plane. But the more I tried to hold back, the more vulnerable I became. I pulled him as close to me as I could, and as I fought to hold on to this moment, I climaxed, and so did he.

We both fell back, spent.

"I love you," I whispered.

"I love you too," he said.

We lay there on the floor for about ten minutes, breathing deep and composing ourselves. Then he propped himself on his forearm. "Baby . . ." he began.

"I know you gotta go." I tried to say it before he did.

"No, I was gonna say, why don't you come back to the hotel with me? You know I need to be there in the morning."

"Okay," I agreed.

"But right now I'm hungry. Let's order in."

That night we ate pizza and hotwings. The television was on, but it was watching us, because we were so into each other, catching up on what we'd missed in each other's lives over the past week. He was so open, and I felt close to him again.

We struggled to keep our eyes open, so we got up and rode in my car over to his hotel, which was only minutes from my place.

"Who brought you to my apartment?" I asked.

"Your brother dropped me off," he said.

"Oh?" At first I worried that I was too transparent. Maurice had been so confident that I'd take him back that he didn't even consider how he was going to get back to his hotel if I didn't. But I chose to cling to the fact that he loved me and he was going to do whatever was necessary to get me back.

Eight

I called Janelle that morning.

"Hey, Anna Mae," I said.

"Hey, girl. What's up?"

"Just wanted to invite you to the game tonight."

"Who's playing?" she asked.

"The Heat and the Hawks."

"Oh, so you're checking up on your ex."

"Actually, he gave me tickets, for your information," I said.

"You're not getting back with him, are you?" she asked, sounding concerned.

"I'm not sure," I said, disappointed that I didn't know. "So, do you want to go?"

"I don't think it will be a good thing for you," Janelle lectured.

"It's only a game. We'll be in the stands, and he'll be on the floor."

"Okay, but only if we can go to the Dance Factory afterward."

"That's cool."

"It should be jumpin' tonight! And I'm due a good time. Corey's been working so hard that we don't get to party much anymore."

"So how are things?" I asked.

"The network is coming along, but our time together is so limited. But quality is better than quantity, right?"

"Right," I agreed. "So meet me here around five. Then we'll meet Maurice for dinner."

"Dinner?"

"Yes, dinner."

"You know you can do much better than him."

"What does dinner have to do with anything? Are you gonna be here?"

"Yes, because I have to watch out for my girl, make sure you're okay."

"Good, I'm glad you've got my back."

"Although I don't want you with him, you need to let him know what he's missing. So be dressed for war because the groupies will be ready to battle. And Maurice needs to know they're no competition for you."

Janelle loved attention and knew how to dress to get it. I, on the other hand, usually wore little makeup and preferred to dress casually and comfortably. Attention on Janelle meant attention on me as well, and every time we went out together I felt like I was on display.

Today I took her advice; after I hung up with her, I went to my brother's spa and got a facial and a roller set. While I sat under the dryer, I was treated to a manicure and pedicure. At home I dressed in a nylon-and-spandex skirt that showed off my long legs. To enhance my upper body, I wore my trusty Wonder Bra underneath a tightly fitted V-neck sweater. My attire, of course, was purchased from sale racks, but my Prada shoes upgraded the look of the entire ensemble. Although I wasn't in the mood to compete, I was ready to do battle.

Janelle was prompt and looking like a supermodel, as usual. Because her parents continued to give her an allowance, she spared no expense when it came to her appearance. She wore a smashing Escada suit and a Giorgio Armani blouse that was unbuttoned low enough to hint at her cleavage. Her makeup was flawless, enhancing her wide-set eyes and newly bleached teeth. And she had just gotten a new weave, so her hair was long, flowing, and full of body. Janelle was ready to meet her awaiting public.

First we went over to the hotel where Maurice was staying and had an early dinner with him in his room. To my surprise he was as attentive toward me as he'd been the night before. When we walked in he gave me a long hug and kiss, and he greeted Janelle as if they were old friends. Once we decided what we'd have sent up from room service, Maurice began to ride Janelle for not hooking up with his friend Ian.

"My man fixed your flat tire and everything, and you shot him down in cold blood when he asked for your number," Maurice said.

"I'm not even gonna entertain this discussion. You know I have a boyfriend."

"Yeah, but has Corey ever gotten on his knees and fixed a flat tire for you?" he joked.

"You're silly," she said. "So, how is Ian?"

"Let's call him," he said. Then he picked up his mobile phone and dialed the number. We took turns talking to Ian. Janelle flirted over the phone, walking to the bathroom to look at herself in the mirror.

Maurice was sitting on his bed, and I walked over to him and sat on his lap. "You look nice," he said.

"Thank you. I was hoping you'd think so."

"Only, don't you think you could have worn something a bit more conservative?" he asked.

"Are you serious?" I laughed.

But he wasn't laughing.

"What's wrong with what I'm wearing?"

"Don't get me wrong, you look really nice. I just think that you should have worn something different for the game, kind of like how Janelle is dressed."

I couldn't believe my ears. Now I would be self-conscious for the rest of the evening. But I wasn't going to let him ruin my night. "Well, we're going out after the game, and what I'm wearing is appropriate for both the game and the club," I said, determined not to let him know just how his words had gotten to me.

"Oh, so you're going out tonight?" he asked sarcastically.

Just then Janelle walked back into the room and passed the phone to Maurice.

"That boy is so funny," she said. "If I wasn't so into Corey, maybe I'd have to give him a chance." Then she rethought her comment. "Nah, I probably wouldn't."

When Janelle looked at me I could see that she knew something was wrong. "You okay?" she mouthed.

I shook my head yeah. Then there was a knock on the door. Janelle went to answer it, and our dinner was served.

• • • •

The Heat beat the Hawks, and just as Janelle predicted, the groupies were out in full force, lurking around after the game. When Maurice came out of the locker room and back into the gym, he was mobbed by men, old and young, children, husbands and wives, and groupies, tons of them, and there was no shame in their persistence. He was one of the new guys, and they wanted to make sure he noticed them. Although I knew this went with the territory it was still annoying, and I thought twice about not waiting around for him. But if I didn't say good-bye, I figured he would've been disappointed. So I waited and waited, and finally got the opportunity to hug him and tell him he had a good game. But something wasn't quite right. There was an emotional wedge between us, I could feel it, but I brushed it off as my own insecurities surfacing.

Our parting was awkward. I didn't want him to leave, but he was a working man, and duty called. He would soon be on the plane, headed to face his next opponent, but I needed to know everything was okay between us. I hated when I got that nagging feeling about our relationship.

Before we walked in separate directions, he said, "See ya, Janelle." Then he looked me over from head to toe and said, "All right then, Nina."

I realized that he didn't want me going to the club. "Maurice, I won't go," I said.

"What are you talking about?" he said, his face blank.

"To the Atlanta Dance Factory. I won't go."

He took a step closer to me. "I'm not trying to stop you from having your fun just to make me happy."

"But I want to make you happy," I said.

"I need to go outside and get on the bus. It's on you," he said, and walked away.

Janelle interrupted me before my emotional battle with myself could begin. "It's time to party. Come on, Nina, let's go get our groove on!"

I attempted to boost my spirit, but I could manage only a dry "Okay, girl, let's go."

.   .   .   .

The Atlanta Dance Factory had a reputation for drawing large crowds and celebrities, and tonight was no exception. As usual there was a ridiculously large group of people waiting in an outrageously long line to get into the club. All celebrities and VIPs walked right in, and the big ballers tipped the doormen anywhere from a hundred to two hundred bucks to cut the long line, and ballers always travel with an entourage, which meant the doormen were making nearly as much as the owners.

We wouldn't be going into the club unless we didn't have to wait in line. The owner was a friend of Corey's, and Janelle had a VIP card. As we walked in the blaring music welcomed us. One of the local radio deejays was spinning hits back-to-back. The energy level was high, and I soon forgot to worry about, what is his name? Oh, yeah, Maurice.

Men in Atlanta can be extremely aggressive. They don't believe in first checking out all the ladies who walk in to see if one really appeals to them, then subtly approaching her. Instead, they make it their business to step to every woman they can to make sure they leave the club with as many phone numbers as possible. It was a numbers game. They were confident that someone would eventually fall for their "What's up, shorty?" pickup line.

We weren't inside for five minutes when we received several offers to dance, or were asked for our phone numbers, or to be some drunken man's bride. More often, we were asked if we wanted anything to drink. Janelle quickly responded to the latter. An older gentleman approached us. His wedding band and dated suit were a dead giveaway that he had been married for some time, but he courageously asked, "Can I buy you two foxy ladies a drink?"

"We're drinking Moët & Chandon," Janelle replied. She is a lady who goes after what she wants and doesn't mind setting standards to weed out undesired company.

"Moët?" the guy said, looking uneasy. "Do you know how much they jack up champagne prices in the club? Oh, so you're trying to break a brother's pockets."

"No, that's not the case," Janelle replied. "We're only drinking that brand of champagne tonight. You offered to pay for our drinks, but if purchasing a bottle of Moët is outside of your budget, that's okay too. Nonetheless, we're drinking Moët."

The gentleman looked embarrassed and stretched out his arms as if to say, "You win some, you lose some," then shook his head, put it down, and walked away. I almost felt sorry for him. Then I noticed that he quickly bounced back and made his way to the next lady who walked by.

There were two levels of VIP here. The first got a hassle-free entrance into the club. The second earned a private area in the back, which required more clout than Janelle's boyfriend had. "You know it's our mission to get into VIP," she said.

"That's cool, but I don't see it happening."

"So, why would we come out if not to party in VIP?"

Janelle's motto was No lines, no commoners (non-VIPs), and no drinks unless they have a nice price tag attached.

"Do I have a choice?" I asked.

"Of course not. Come on, girl," she said and walked toward VIP as if we belonged there.

We of course were met by a security guard who didn't look friendly, or the least bit interested in why we felt like we belonged in

VIP. I for one was not in the mood to be embarrassed, but I knew that the only way Janelle was leaving the club was through VIP.

Before I got the opportunity to watch her work her magic, two players for the Atlanta Braves walked up with some of their friends and spoke to me. One of them was a client of my brother's, and I had met him a few times at the spa.

"Hey, Nina, is it?" he asked.

"Yes, it is. How are you?" I extended my hand. We shook.

"We're doing our thing. It's our partner's birthday and we're celebrating." He introduced us to the birthday boy and the rest of his crew.

"So, are you and your friend headed for VIP?" the other player, Tim, asked. He was really checking out Janelle.

"We don't exactly—" I began.

"We'd love to join you," Janelle said, grabbing him by the arm.

And we walked in, no problem.

The VIP area was another party within itself, consisting of a private deejay, hors d'oeuvres, and extremely attentive waitresses wearing skimpy uniforms. It held up to its reputation that night, boasting several athletes, a few actresses, and the Atlanta stars Jermaine Dupree, TLC, Too Short, and Toni Braxton. Everybody seemed to be letting loose. I scanned the room and noticed even more celebrity faces.

"So, would you ladies like to join us at our table?" Tim asked Janelle.

"Sure we would," she replied.

"Could you come here for a second?" I asked, interrupting her bliss. "Now, I know you're ready to mingle, but we both have boyfriends and this scene could be misconstrued and get back as an unnecessary scandal."

"Lighten up," she said. "Nobody knows us, so just relax and don't get too close, especially to that Tim. He's mine tonight." She laughed and cozied herself into the seat next to him.

"So, what are you ladies drinking?" Tim asked. "How about champagne? After all, this is supposed to be a celebration."

Janelle looked across the table at me and winked, then flashed a wicked grin, as if to say, "I told you we're drinking Moët tonight!"

The waitress brought out two bottles of champagne and several glasses. We toasted the birthday boy, and I made small talk with several of the guys at the table about sports. Janelle snuggled up to her new friend.

A couple of the guys at the table attempted to get too friendly. I gave Janelle the "It's time for you to get or give the digits because we need to move on" look. She caught the hint.

The tough thing about being an upwardly mobile, attractive African-American woman in this day is that you can easily be labeled a groupie if you obtain too much access to party with celebrities but aren't seriously involved with one in particular, or not working within the industry. Little things like that bother me. I was so aware of eyes watching Janelle and me as we made our way to the ladies' room. Janelle seemed to enjoy the attention. I could imagine people thinking, or, even worse, saying to one another, "I wonder who those groupies will be leaving the club with tonight."

Janelle always says, "You only have to answer to two people, Nina—yourself and God." I repeated that advice to myself all the way to the ladies' room.

"He wants to take me to the movies next week," Janelle yelled enthusiastically as we walked toward the mirror, past the line of women waiting for an available stall.

"I'm ready to leave," I blurted. Where'd that come from?

"What?" Janelle asked, almost as if she'd heard my request but didn't want to.

"I'm ready to take off these overpriced shoes and slip into some sweats and watch TV until I fall asleep." I did want to go home, yet I knew I wouldn't be able to sleep because I had this nagging feeling that things would become rocky again between me and the man I felt so deeply for.

"You must be insane. We just got here."

"I wouldn't normally argue with you, but I'm not feeling it tonight. I don't feel like networking. I don't feel like mingling. I don't even want to dance." I could feel my voice escalating, so I lowered it. "Plus, you've achieved your mission for the night. You got to drink a few glasses of nice champagne, and even though it wasn't part of your strategy, one of the richest men in the club has asked you out. Can we please leave?"

"You know, you're right," she said, then pulled a comb out of her purse and began grooming her hair. "Plus I need to get my beauty rest. I'm going to a seminar tomorrow, and I have to wake up early."

"You are? What kind of seminar?"

"It's about choosing the right career."

"Why didn't you tell me? I would have planned to go with you."

"Nina, everybody knows what's right for you: journalism," she said. "But I majored in sociology. This is one time I have to say my parents were right, I should have had a more concentrated major. Now I have to make a mature career decision and figure out what I really want to do, even if it means going back to school."

"Whoa!"

"Girl, things are not getting any better at the office. I can't work for that woman anymore, and I will not be an administrative assistant for the rest of my life."

"I hear you," I said. I took the comb from Janelle's hand and began touching up my own hairdo.

"I was thinking about taking some business classes," she said casually, while pulling out powder and lipstick from her purse. "Who knows, maybe I'd have a better opportunity of moving up the corporate ladder. Or maybe I'll start my own business."

I was pleased to hear that Janelle was taking steps to improve her stagnant career. I needed to do the same, but right now I couldn't think about that. I had to get home so I could try to figure out how to keep my failing relationship intact.

Janelle lightly powdered her face. "Girl, that Tim is fine," she said. "I like his style."

"I'm telling Corey," I joked.

"So!" she responded. "Anyway, Corey's out of town."

I left it alone, because I knew that as flattered as Janelle was that

Tim had asked her out, she wouldn't go through with it—she was in love with Corey.

"Can we go?" I requested.

"All right."

After Janelle made sure she was perfect she said to me, "I know you like a book, and I know you're worried about Maurice. Stop stressing. Whatever is to be will be, and worrying won't change anything."

Her words of wisdom were well received, and we walked through the crowd of haves and want-to-haves in VIP, then through the commoners and out to Janelle's candy-apple red Mitsubishi Eclipse.

. . . .

I was in front of my parents' bedroom door and I could hear my father screaming at my mother. "I wish I'd never never married you! My life has been a living hell with you in it!"

"Please, Smitty, don't say that," she said.

I tried to open the door and save my mother, but it was locked.

I shook the door and my dad's voice escalated. Then I could hear bumping and thudding, and furniture being knocked around. He was beating her. I knew. I pushed against the door with all my might. When it opened I was at the Atlanta Dance Factory, only it was smaller. I was sitting at the bar sipping a glass of wine. An attractive, cleanly dressed gentleman walked up to me, and we began to talk. I was enjoying the conversation. When I looked over my shoulder I noticed Maurice standing in the middle of the dance floor. He waved his hand, and I turned away from the guy beside me and began to walk toward Maurice. The closer I got to him, the farther away he seemed, so I walked faster, but the faster I walked, the larger the room became. When I tried to focus on Maurice again, he turned into my father. I awoke, overcome with the strangest feeling of loneliness. I thought of calling Maurice but decided instead to turn on some soothing jazz and take a long hot bath.

Nine

"Nina!" Mom yelled to me. "Will you come and help your aging mother set the table?" I had been at my parents' house for about ten minutes when Janelle called. She couldn't wait to tell me about the date she'd had with Tim the previous night. I was shocked that she'd gone through with it.

"Okay, Mom," I yelled. "I'll be right there—give me five minutes." It was Christmas Eve, and Mom had requested that Brice and I come for dinner. We would spend the night and have Christmas breakfast, go to the sunrise church service, then come back and exchange gifts. Brice had invited Brianna.

"What's up?" I asked Janelle.

"You know I have to fill you in on all the juicy details from last night."

"Girl, you are out of control."

"I know. Isn't it great?"

"What movie did you see?" I asked.

"Well, we went out to eat first at this nice seafood restaurant in Buckhead. The food was great. Then, instead of going to a late movie, we decided to go back to his place and take a dip in his Jacuzzi."

"Whose idea was that?" I asked. My best friend went out with a star baseball player and was acting like a groupie. I didn't want her to acquire that kind of negative label, and I surely didn't want it rubbing off on me and affecting my future as a sports journalist.

"His, of course. I didn't even know he had a Jacuzzi. Well, I could have assumed. But who can be sure?"

"I'm not surprised. Wanted to flex and show off his place? He seemed like the type."

"Yeah, and understandably so. He lives in Alpharetta, and Nina, his house is the kind of place I could see myself living in. It's so elegant."

"Girl, you are crazy! What about Corey, and why are you talking about moving in with Tim?"

"I said I could see myself in that house," she said defensively. "I didn't say with whom! I'm beginning to believe you have dual personalities. When you're involved in a serious relationship you become Miss Goody Two-shoes. I like you better when you're single. Call me when you and Maurice get a divorce." She said it jokingly, but it was true. In each of my relationships I've been very committed.

"I'm not paying you any attention," I replied.

"That's the problem," she said. "You know I'm attention-starved."

"Tell me about it!" We laughed.

"Girl, I spent the night with him!" Janelle screamed through the telephone.

"You had sex with him?"

"No, I only spent the night. I mean, we kissed a lot and teased a little, but sex, no. I'm on my period."

"Gross," I said. "That's a bit more information than I needed!" It was bad enough that she was cheating, but that "easy" routine wasn't the route to take with most athletes who have sex thrown at them on a daily basis. "So, what's your plan with him? I thought you were hoping to settle down with Corey."

"What do you mean, my plan? I just wanted to have a good time."

"But what about Corey?"

"I didn't say anything before, Nina, maybe because I've been in denial," she said, then paused. "I have spent very little time with Corey over the last several months. We used to at least have meaningful conversations over the phone, but lately he's been so busy trying to get the network off the ground that even our telephone calls have lost their spark."

"That's not an excuse, Janelle." I know she wanted my approval of her spending the night with Tim, but I couldn't give it. "Why don't you just break up with him?"

"It's not that simple Nina. I'm hoping Corey will eventually get the ball rolling and soon have time for me. But until then, I realize that I'm human and I need affection and attention."

"But did you have to stay with Tim?" I asked.

"Yes, because that's what I felt like doing," she said sternly.

"Well, if you feel like you want to lie in the bed with someone else, you need to break up with Corey, period," I said firmly. I couldn't believe my best friend was acting like the men in my life—like Brice and Dad and Maurice. I had to bring her back to her senses. "Deep down you know you're moving too fast with Tim."

"Yeah, you're probably right, but you only live once."

"Again, that's no excuse."

"So why are you jumping on my case?" she asked.

"Because you're my friend and I don't want you to mess up what you have with Corey."

"He's the one who's messing up," she said. "It's Christmas Eve. Do you think my phone has rung?"

"Look. I'm out of it." Obviously I wasn't getting anywhere with her.

"Good!" she said with a bitter edge to her voice.

"So, when are you seeing him again?" I asked.

"I thought you were out of it?"

"You don't have to answer me."

"Not sure," she replied.

"Do you want to?"

"Of course!"

"All right, Anna Mae. Well, keep me posted. I'd better get in there and help Mom. You know how she gets about her holiday dinners."

"Of course I do. So when is she gonna invite me over again?"

"She's not!" I joked. "You eat too much!"

"Last night Tim thought my healthy appetite was sexy!"

"I just bet he did."

"And if he thought I was sexy last night, he should see me chowing down on your mother's cooking," she joked.

"You're so crazy!"

"I know!" she replied. "But I'd better go downstairs and see what my own mother is cooking. See you tomorrow evening?"

"Yeah, let's exchange gifts and do a Christmas slumber party at my place."

"Okay. So I guess that means you're still my friend?" Janelle asked.

"Just because I don't approve of your extracurricular activities doesn't mean I'm gonna disown you."

"Good, because I need you to be my conscience."

"Merry Christmas!" I said.

"Merry Christmas!" she replied.

•   •   •   •

The house glowed with a festive Christmas decor, which Mom and I had labored to create earlier in the week. We covered the place with garlands, little white lights, red bows, and silver trimmings. The dinner table was beautifully set. Brice, Brianna, and I were in the basement watching a basketball game. I was scouting new talent. I loved predicting the next breakout player. Brice watched intently and Brianna attempted to seem interested, although it was obvious she was clueless about the sport. Momma was in the kitchen fussing over the final touches to dinner. Daddy still hadn't made it in. Momma had said earlier that he stopped by a friend's house and said he'd be home for dinner. But somehow I knew she wasn't telling the truth about his whereabouts.

At the commercial break I went back into the kitchen. "Momma, is dinner ready yet?"

"Yeah, and no thanks to you. I can't believe how you get into those sports, just like a man. If you weren't seeing Maurice, I'd be a little worried about you, if you know what I mean."

Ignoring the latter comment, I complained, "I prepared the salad and set the table. What did Brice do?"

"He's a man."

"And?" I asked. My mother was so old-fashioned. I am too, in some ways, but she goes overboard.

"It just wouldn't be right. Plus he has company."

I didn't want to debate with her. For one, I knew it wouldn't get me anywhere, but there was something else too. I noticed how tired my mother was looking lately. It was obvious that either she hadn't been getting any sleep or that she'd been crying. I wanted to help her, but I didn't know how. So instead of lending words of encouragement I tried to piss her off, hoping that if she got mad enough, she would confront my father once and for all—or at the very least share with me what was going on with her. "So, Momma, where did you say Daddy went to visit?"

"He had to pick up something from the nursery."

"I thought you said earlier he was visiting with a friend." I hated when she tried to cover for Dad.

"Well, Nina, if you already knew where he was, why did you ask again?" she snapped.

"It's just that dinner is nearly done, and I was wondering if he'd be here on time." I didn't want to say what I was really thinking: Tell the truth, Momma. He didn't come in last night. He stayed with his girlfriend. But we had company, and I didn't want to cause a scene, so I kept silent.

"Hey, hey, hey!" I heard my daddy's voice from the family room.

"Hey, Dad!" my brother said. "You remember Brianna, don't you?"

"Yeah, I do. How ya doing, Brianna?"

"Fine, thank you. Just ready to eat some of your wife's good cooking."

"Ditto that," my dad replied. "Something's sure smelling good in here," he said as he walked through the hall and into the kitchen.

"Nina, hey, pumpkin." He seemed surprised to see me. "I haven't seen you in weeks. Where's Maurice this weekend?"

I used to be so excited to see my dad. I would run to him and hug him and give him a big kiss on the cheek. But I couldn't bring myself to do so anymore. I felt like my mom needed an ally in this situation. "Hey, Dad! He flew into L.A. today. He has a game there tomorrow."

"You find a new job yet?"

"I have a job," I responded.

"I mean a better-paying job," he complained.

"Not yet." I walked over to the oven, where my mother was standing.

"You keep looking," he said, then looked over at my mother, who was busying herself at the stove. "So how you doing, Juanita?" he asked. I sensed guilt screaming through the subtle question.

She looked over her shoulder and replied, "I'm just finishing up with dinner. Why don't y'all all go and wash up and we'll eat in the dining room." Then she walked past him without looking him in the face and yelled into the basement, "Come on, Brice and Brianna, get washed up. It's time to eat."

"Music to my ears," Brice shouted back. I could hear the movement from the other room. Meanwhile, my father stood silently, looking at the food on the stove. It was Christmas Eve, and neither of my parents bothered truly acknowledging the other.

If he's so guilty and feels so bad, why doesn't he change or divorce her? I mean, I know men cheat, but when it gets to this point, they have to take responsibility for their actions, ask for a divorce, something. I know my dad can't be trying to protect my mother's feelings, because if he was, he wouldn't stay out all night and he would treat her as an equal and with honor and love. And if his intention was not to hurt her, then he was just too late, because although I can't describe it, the energy coming from my mom was something deeper than hurt.

And Janelle, I couldn't believe that she had fallen by the wayside. I thought I had an ally with all women in the stand for monogamy and respect within relationships. But my main girl had let me down. Maybe I was just disillusioned. Maybe nobody cared anymore.

Ten

Maurice called the day before New Year's Eve. I was still lounging in bed in my pajamas reading a novel when the phone rang. "Hey, baby," he said.

"Maurice?"

"Of course, baby. What's going on? You miss me?"

"You know I do."

"Listen, there's going to be a New Year's Eve party there in Atlanta. I want to stay with you and we can go to the party together. Is that cool?"

"Well, I made plans to go with Janelle to—"

"Oh, so you don't want to see me. You always saying you want to spend time, and when you get the opportunity you go and bring up Janelle's name."

"No, I'm just saying that—"

"Forget it. I'll just check into a hotel and go to the party by my damn self," he said, his temper beginning to flare. It seemed that every time we talked I walked a thin line. If I said the wrong thing, like mentioning how well someone else on his team played, or asked when we would see each other again, he would get testy. I quickly learned to let him lead our conversations. I wanted a peaceful relationship, and being cautious with my words was worth the effort.

"Maurice, wait." I had to stop him before he hung up. "What Janelle and I had planned isn't important. I was going to say that we were going to go to the Underground to watch the peach drop, but if you're coming, that plan is history," I said, softening my voice. "So when will you be here?"

"Tomorrow morning, but you don't have to go with me," he said, a hint of edginess still in his tone.

"You know I'd be a fool not to want to go with you. I can't wait to see you. We've got a lot of catching up to do."

"Go ahead and invite Janelle and Brice and their dates. Maybe Janelle can invite that guy she's all in love with, what's his name?" he asked, minus the chip. My ego stroking worked.

"Corey," I replied. "But I'm not sure if he's gonna make it."

"Whatever, it's all good either way."

It often amazed me how easily he switched from angry to friendly. "Okay. Will I need to pick you up from the airport?" I asked.

"No need. I'll be at your apartment around eleven-thirty A.M. And ask your brother if he can hook up my fade."

"Okay. So what's the dress code for the party?"

"Just look pretty for me," he said.

"Is it formal, cosmo, casual?"

"I don't know. Just look pretty."

"Okay," I replied, realizing that I wasn't going to get a clear answer from him. "Where's the party going to be?"

"At the Ritz."

"Downtown or Buckhead?"

"I'm not sure," he said casually.

I hung up the phone and immediately called both Ritz Carlton hotels and got the information for the party. It would be a formal affair at the downtown location. I should have guessed. Now I would have to buy something to wear with the money I got from my parents for Christmas. That money was supposed to be added to my savings account. I'm dating a millionaire and breaking the bank to keep up. I should have asked him to buy me a dress for the occasion, but I didn't dare. My mother always told me never to ask a man for anything, because when he starts giving, he feels like he owns you. And I didn't want Maurice to have that kind of power over me. He was already tough enough to handle as it was.

I called my brother and begged him to squeeze Maurice into their New Year's Eve schedule. He agreed only after I invited him to the party. He hadn't planned anything for him and Brianna and was relieved that they now had something to do.

Then I called Janelle's apartment, but I didn't get an answer, so I tried her mobile phone. She picked up. "Hello." She sounded stressed.

"Are you okay?"

"No, I'm on my way over to see you. Just let me park, and I'll be up."

A few minutes later I buzzed Janelle in and heard her stomp her way up the stairs. When I opened the door, she walked right by me and began venting.

"And you asked why I went out with Tim. To keep my sanity! I refuse to be strung along. I am a woman, and I will be treated as such. I cannot put that much time into a relationship and have a man be so casual about my importance."

"What happened?" I asked, closing the door to avoid disturbing the neighbors any further.

Janelle was usually even-tempered, but extremely opinionated and what I've always called "aware." The inconsiderate or underhanded things that people did never seemed to shock her. Janelle always liked to feel in control of her fate. She always had some phrase that justified why she shouldn't allow herself to be fazed. I've only seen her moved to anger by two people: her boss and Corey.

"I had to break up with him. Nina, I've been patient. You know that, but there is no way I'm going to go through this holiday season without seeing Corey and remain his girlfriend. There's not that much work for him to do, come on. I mean, really."

"When did you talk to him?"

"Today," she said, finally calming herself enough to take a seat on my sofa.

I sat down beside her. "Over the phone or in person?"

"Do you think he'd be considerate enough to see me in person?" she complained. "I'm thirsty. What do you have?"

I walked into the kitchen and opened the refrigerator. "I have bottled water, fruit juice, and Coke."

"Water," she requested, then went back to her arraignment. "And I thought Corey was different. I fell for the fact that he was ambitious, intelligent, self-made. And he was always a gentleman in the beginning. But he's just like . . . I was going to say all men, but I refuse to believe that all men are as inconsiderate and self-centered as Corey."

I wasn't sure I was up to hearing any disappointing news about a man today. It seemed that I couldn't escape it. Although Maurice was fine today, I knew it was subject to change without notice. I sympathized with Janelle. I liked Corey, but his being unavailable, especially during the holiday, was a bit much. I shouldn't have been surprised by her decision, but I wondered if she was being a bit hasty. "Did you give him the opportunity to explain?" I asked her.

"What is there to explain?" She took the glass of water from me and sipped. "I asked him what he planned for New Year's Eve. He said sleeping because he'd be working all day and would want to start the new year on the right foot, by doing more work."

"So, he's committed to his job. You've always known that."

"Then he had the nerve to say, 'You can come over late and spend the night.' " Her arms began flying again. "Can you believe he had the guts to suggest a booty call? Nina, I didn't get a Christmas gift, a Merry Christmas, Happy Kwanzaa, nothing. He didn't call. Then he had the nerve to want me to sex him up. He's got another thing coming."

"I hear you, Anna Mae."

"So I had no other choice but to break up with him." Janelle fell back and sunk into the couch. "You know what's so pitiful? I still love him and I want the network to be a success, but I love myself more. I mean, I have needs." There was a strength behind her misery. I knew she was serious. It was definitely an end for her and Corey, and there would be no turning back. When Janelle made a decision, good or bad, she usually stuck by it, if for no other reason than to prove to herself it was right.

"Yeah," I said.

"I'd like to be told that I'm beautiful. I need to know he realizes I'm special. I never asked for quantity time. Just occasional time. He couldn't even give that."

I refrained from commenting because I understood her position and admired her strength to let go of the relationship because it wasn't working for her. I was different, determined to make my relationship last at any cost. I believed in sacrificing for love. So any advice that I would have given would have been in vain.

I remained silent and allowed her to justify her decision to leave Corey and reaffirm herself as a woman.

"I'd rather be lonely by myself than lonely with someone. I am a college graduate! I am smart and beautiful. Corey is an ignorant fool to let me slip away. If he can't appreciate all that I have to offer, it's his loss! And the bastard had better find out a way to be able to hold on to that network at night because he'll never touch my beautiful body again!"

By the time she got off her pedestal, she was more sure of her decision than ever.

Eleven

Janelle and Tim met Maurice and me at my apartment, then Brice and Brianna swung by in a rented limousine to pick all of us up. The driver buzzed, and we filed down the stairs into the cool Atlanta winter air. In the limo, Janelle introduced Tim around, and we were off. Brice cracked open a bottle of wine.

"Let's toast to appreciating the finer things in life, letting go of the old, and embracing the blessing of today," Brice said, and winked at Brianna. She winked back. We touched glasses and cheered.

"Why don't we share our resolutions?" I suggested. "I'll start. I'm not gonna go down the whole list, but one is to be more understanding." I directed this at Maurice. I wanted him to know that despite anything he'd done to me in the past, I believed we could start fresh and build a solid relationship.

"I have to go with Brice's toast," Janelle said. "Can I steal that as my own resolution?"

"Oh, no doubt!" Brice said.

"That and cutting down on my shopping. I've got to do better!"

"Here, here!" I said, and we touched glasses.

"What's your resolution?" Janelle asked Tim.

"Okay, here goes. I want to be a better person. I've done some dirt in my time, believe me, and my resolution is to do a few things differently. You know?"

"I hear you, man. That's deep," Brice said. They touched glasses. The car got quiet. Brice nudged Brianna. "Okay, baby, bring it on."

"I gotta go with the overused; I need to get in the gym and eat healthier. I may even start juicing."

"That's cool, as long as you don't try to force me to go the healthy route with you. I'm down with the workout, but I don't think I'm quite ready for juicing."

We laughed.

"All right, Maurice, man, it's on you to bring up the rear," Brice said.

"Man, I don't really have any resolutions, other than trying to up my game. You know, score more. That's about it."

"We'll take that!" I said.

"That's definitely one of mine," Tim added.

"Oh, yeah," Brice chimed in. "I want to do the same with the spa, up my game. Improve. Maybe expand, who knows. The sky's the limit on New Year's Eve."

We clinked glasses all around. The mood was festive, and everyone seemed happy and excited. The plan was to party through to the new year, and once our feet couldn't move anymore, we'd leave the party and go to a greasy, twenty-four-hour breakfast spot.

Tim and Brice hit it off. Maurice was cold to Tim, and geared his comments to everyone except him. I don't know what his problem with Tim was, but Tim didn't seem to be affected by Maurice's rude behavior.

We walked into the party, and there were hostesses at the door handing out favors. It was a mixed crowd of industry heads and celebrities, the typical exclusive Atlanta party of the rich and famous. I locked my arm around Maurice's and scanned the room to get a feel for my surroundings. There were candlelit tables surrounding a stage and dance floor. A band was performing, and before I could figure out who they were, Maurice jerked my arm. "Who are you looking at?" he demanded.

"I'm just looking around," I said, confused.

"You don't need to be looking at nobody in here, except me," he shot back. "And stay away from Tim."

"Why?" I asked.

"That brother was looking at you too hard while we were in the limo. I started to say something, but I'm gonna chill."

"He was not."

"Don't start with me, Nina. I know what I saw."

Before I could absorb this exchange, a well-dressed lady ran over to Maurice and gave him a welcome hug, then began to small talk. She completely ignored me, and Maurice didn't bother to introduce us. I took a deep breath and tried to overlook the incident. Finally the woman moved on. I refused to stoop to Maurice's level and complain about a mere conversation with someone who was insignificant as far as I was concerned. I wanted to enjoy myself.

This kind of affair was right up Janelle's alley. She loved glitz and glamour, and being at an exclusive party with an accomplished athlete was just the medicine she needed to help ease the hurt of her breakup with Corey. She strutted to our table in true diva fashion. Our dates seated us and then themselves. From here I was able to recognize the band; it was the Isley Brothers. They were playing "Who's That Lady," and Ron Isley was blowing the crowd away. I felt lucky to be here with my boyfriend, except that I was uncomfortable looking around— I didn't want to upset Maurice by making him feel insecure—so I didn't. It had been a while since we'd been in public together, and I hadn't remembered him being so concerned about me checking out other men.

Brianna and Brice were whispering in each other's ears and laughing. Janelle and Tim were snapping their fingers and moving to the music. Tim escorted her to the floor, and they began grooving. I noticed Maurice bobbing his head, so I leaned over and asked him to dance. He didn't respond. "Come on." I smiled and gave him a nudge. He smiled back, and we headed to the floor. Brice and Brianna were right behind. I was feeling wonderful. I had my man, my brother, and my best friend with me to celebrate a new year.

Maurice and I danced, smiling and staring deeply into each

other's eyes. The connection between us was intense, despite the occasional drama. "I love you," I said.

"Ditto that," he replied, and kissed my cheek.

Brice started playing the switch game, and we each traded dance partners. Then he yelled switch again, and he and I were dancing together. "What do you think about Brianna?" he asked me. I was taken aback, because he'd never cared what I thought about any of his girlfriends in the past.

"She's nice," I answered. "I'm just surprised that you've been with one 'lady' for so long."

"I think I love her," he said.

"Switch!" Tim took over Brice's job, then we switched again, back to our original partners.

I had never once heard Brice express love for anybody. He'd said that he cared, or that he loved having sex with, or that he liked being around individual women, but he'd never talked about love. Watching him with Brianna, I saw now there was something different about him with her. He did love her. It was obvious. How had I missed it? I guess I'd been too preoccupied with my own relationships, or my parents, to notice. I wasn't even sure if she was a good match for Brice. I had never taken the time to get to know her because I grouped her with all the others—I thought he would have dropped her for someone else by now, so why bother?

The Isleys slowed things down, while Ron Isley cooed "Woo! We gonna sing it all tonight, y'all. Taking you straight into the new year. Woo!" They began playing "Groove with You." Maurice pulled me close to him, and we moved with the music. Although I don't think he was ever comfortable dancing in public, Maurice was a good dancer. I rested my head on his chest and enjoyed the music and our closeness.

We were having a ball. Janelle, Brianna, and I were walking over to the hors d'oeuvre table when a handsome gentleman walked up to me and put his arms around my waist. I was stunned. I had no idea who this stranger was and why he was hugging me. And I didn't want Maurice to get the wrong impression.

"Hey, Nina," he said.

"Do I know you?" I asked. He had long brown dreadlocks that were neatly pulled back with a tie. I didn't know anybody with dreads that fondly.

"You don't remember me," he said, surprised.

"Leonard Jones!" Janelle screamed, "Oh my God, Nina, it's LJ Love!"

"Leo," I said.

"Oh, so you do remember," he said in a sexy deep voice. This was not the Leo Jay I remembered from high school.

"Hey, Leonard, we saw you on BET," Janelle said. "Well, I saw you and I told Nina about it."

Leo smiled. "Hey, Janelle, you haven't changed a bit." Then he turned his attention to me. "So, Nina, are you visiting for the holidays?"

"Actually, I moved back after graduation," I replied. Then I turned away from him, grabbed a plate, and began to pile it with fruit, veggies, and meatballs. I could feel Maurice's eyes on me from across the room. I didn't want my conversation with Leo to last much longer. I was hoping he would get the picture, but he followed me, grabbing a plate himself.

"Nina, you're still as beautiful as you were in school," he said shyly. That was the Leo I remembered.

I smiled. "Thank you." Then I took a deep breath; I was getting nervous. I didn't want to be rude, but I needed Leo to be as far away from me as possible before the scene turned ugly.

He must have picked up on my discomfort, because he said, "Hey, I'm sure you're here with someone else, and I don't want to offend the lucky brother. I just wanted to get a closer look at you, if only one more time." He smiled. Even though I was worried about Maurice, I couldn't help but notice that Leo was all man. He had grown up and was attractive, confident, appealing, but there was still a trace of that timid teenager asking me to sign his yearbook.

"Yes, I'm here with my boyfriend," I replied.

"Well, here, take my card, and if you ever need anything, even just to talk, give me a call."

"Leo, I can't," I began.

"Listen, it doesn't take a brain surgeon to figure out that you're not available, but I'm extending my friendship whenever or if ever you may need it." He placed the card on the table and walked away. I quickly grabbed it and put it in my purse, then looked around to see if Maurice was watching from the table. His seat was empty.

I looked over at Janelle, and she watched Leo walk away. "You just never know about a person, do you?" she said. "Judge not, lest ye be judged." She shook her head. "I must have been blind in high school to have missed that."

"We all were," I commented. When I looked up Maurice was standing before me.

"Who the hell was that?" he asked.

"Maurice, relax," Janelle interrupted. "It was just—"

"This has nothing to do with you, Janelle," he snapped.

Janelle stepped back but didn't remove her eyes from us.

"Like I said, what's up, Nina? Is that your new boyfriend?" He moved closer to me, hemming me in against the table.

Brianna and Janelle watched, with looks of shock on their faces.

"Maurice, he was just a guy that Janelle and I went to high school with."

"So why was he talking to you? I bring my lady out to a nice party, and she has the nerve to front on me and play Maurice like I'm some chump."

"What do you mean?" I asked.

"Just don't say nothing to me for the rest of the night," he said, and stormed off.

"But Maurice," I begged, and chased after him. When I caught up, he was huffing, so I knew he wouldn't listen to anything I said, but I had to try. "Baby, I wasn't even really talking to him," I said, trying to grab his arm. He jerked away.

"Don't touch me."

I quickly let go. "I tried to ignore him, but he kept talking, I promise," I pleaded. But he paid no attention to me. My face felt flushed. Leo's timing was horrible, and my heart was aching for a peaceful night out with Maurice. I hated that feeling, but I couldn't calm myself. "Maurice, it's almost midnight. Please don't be angry with me."

"If you don't get out of my face, I promise I'll knock you to the floor with all my might. And I'm sure you don't want to bring any more embarrassment to yourself than you already have."

I frowned and stepped back. Everything was falling apart, and it suddenly felt like everybody in the place was watching me.

"Listen," he said. "I don't want this anymore. I won't be riding back with you tonight. I'll come over before I fly out tomorrow and get my things. Just have them by the door because I don't have nothing else to say to you." He turned around and walked toward the men's room.

Janelle and Brianna rushed over to me. "I can't believe he's being so immature," Janelle said. "Forget him."

"Yeah, you would say that," I returned. I was furious. She had no right to comment. She didn't know how I was feeling. When Maurice walked away, my heart broke once again. Why did he have to ruin everything? I knew he didn't mean what he said; it was just his way of releasing his pent-up anger. Everything would be okay in the morning, I told myself.

We walked back over to the table, and before long Ron Isley was preparing the crowd for the countdown to the new year. "Yeah, yeah," he sang.

The crowd yelled back. "Yeah, yeah, oh, yeah," they yelled louder.

"I feel all right," he crooned. "I feel all right. I feeeeeel all right."

"Where's Maurice?" Brice asked.

I shrugged. I was in agony. I couldn't bear to talk or I would cry, and I wasn't about to cry into the new year.

Ron continued to introduce the upcoming song. "You don't know like I know what she's done for me. Oh yeah, I feel all all right. I'm gonna take you all the way back to 1959." He paused for the response. The crowd yelled and clapped.

"Is everybody ready?" Ron shouted. "Stand up, y'all. Grab your lady 'cause we've got one more minute until the clock strikes twelve. So get on your feet, 'cause we gonna celebrate!"

The band roused up and began to play the song "Shout." "You know it makes me want to shout!" Everybody in the audience was out of their chairs dancing and having a blast. Tim and Brice pulled their dates to the floor. Janelle and Brianna looked back at me, as if to apologize, but it wasn't their fault that my boyfriend's explosions couldn't be contained for a more appropriate time.

I sat in my seat and wondered what I would do with myself when they announced the new year in less than a minute. I couldn't just sit there solo at the table, and my pride wouldn't allow me to go on the dance floor with the two happy couples. I tapped the table with my nails and began to panic. My mother always said, watch what you're doing at the stroke of New Year's, because odds are you'll be doing that very thing for the rest of the year. I certainly didn't want to be alone with my heartache for the rest of the year. Before I could stop myself, I stood up and walked quickly toward the men's room. I heard Ron Isley begin the countdown, and my feet moved faster. I caught a glimpse of the girl who'd spoken to Maurice earlier. She was at a table of women who had stood up on their seats and were blowing their party blowers. LJ Love was at a table nearby, pouring champagne into people's glasses. Everyone seemed happy and free, while I was chasing after love.

By the time I finally made it to the men's room, the countdown was over and everyone was yelling Happy New Year. Balloons and confetti fell from the ceiling, and people were hugging and kissing. Although I tried to contain them, tears were streaming from my eyes as I pushed open the men's room door. Maurice was inside, alone, leaning against the counter. The joyful noise of the celebration poured inside, but Maurice seemed impervious. His arms were crossed, and he stared at me, expressionless.

"I'm sorry." I was still weeping as I walked toward him and put my arms around him. He didn't budge. He didn't hug me back.

A lump formed in my throat. I needed his love, and I wasn't going to walk out of that rest room without it. I began to kiss his face, his lips, his neck. Still no response.

"Maurice," I pleaded. "Please don't do this to me. I can't handle you being so cold."

Nothing.

Going limp, I laid my head on his chest and bawled like a hungry baby. The door swung open, and the attendant walked in and saw us. "Sir, ma'am, you can't be in here like this." I just squeezed Maurice tighter. I wasn't leaving without him.

"Nina," Maurice said.

I didn't answer.

"Nina." He paused. He leaned over the counter, got a tissue and handed it to me. After I dried my face, he stroked my chin and grinned mildly. "Let's go," he said. He reached into his pocket and tipped the attendant fifty dollars, put his arms around me, and we walked out into the ballroom. People were still cheering as we made our way back to the table. I had my man and was having my own internal celebration. But behind the celebration was a nagging thought, one I kept pushing to the back of my mind: that Maurice would continue to take from me emotionally and give only when he was certain I was below empty.

Twelve

One of my New Year's resolutions was to get a new job, either with CNN Sports or at another network. I mailed out several résumés and kept my eyes open for positions within my department. I had a new long-term temp job with CNN, as an administrative assistant. There was nothing about the work that utilized my degree and it gave me no job satisfaction, but I was going to begin anew and give 100 percent until my first break came along.

At first work was a breeze. I was fifteen minutes early every day, and I completed assignments in record time. One day in February I checked my home voice mail from the office during my lunch break. There was a message from Maurice. I could tell by his tone that something wasn't quite right, so I phoned him immediately. He wasn't home and wasn't picking up his mobile phone, so I left messages on each, then replayed his message to me to try and decipher what it was I'd heard in his tone. I was distracted for the rest of the afternoon, and five o'clock couldn't come soon enough.

I attempted to reach Maurice all weekend, to no avail. He finally called Sunday evening. By then I was frantic.

"Maurice, where have you been?" I asked. "I got your message and tried to call all weekend. Is everything all right?"

"I was busy," he replied calmly.

"Why didn't you answer your cell? You usually have it on."

"I don't know. What are you doing?"

"I'm worried about you."

"Other than that?"

"Well, I'm going through the classifieds, looking for new opportunities to send out more résumés."

"Oh!" There was silence.

"So, what did you want to talk to me about?" I asked.

He took a deep breath. "Nina, we've been together for what, almost seven months?"

"Eight," I corrected him. "It's been since June." It occurred to me that he sounded a bit nervous, and that maybe he wanted to ask me to marry him. But no, it was too soon.

"Well, yeah, we've been seeing each other for eight months," he said. "A few more and it would be a full year."

"Right."

"That's a lot of time to be with one person."

"That depends on what you consider a lot of time," I said. Where was he going with this?

"And it's tougher when there's distance between two people."

"You're right, it can be. So what are you saying?" I was getting nervous. Maybe he really *was* going to propose.

"Well, Nina, the distance is getting to me, and I don't see no way around it. I know I'm not ready to get married—I'm too young. And I can't have a woman living with me out of wedlock. My mother would go ballistic."

"Maurice, what are you saying?" An aching began to creep into my heart. I knew what was coming next.

"You know what I'm saying, Nina."

"Please don't do this to me. Not now! Please, Maurice, we can work this out."

"I've been thinking about this for some time, and I'm through trying. It's just not worth it."

"What's not? Me? Us?"

"The distance, Nina. I'm on the road a lot as it is. And when I come back into town, you're not there. Calling you on the phone is not the same as having you here."

"Maurice, don't give up on us that easily. I love you and I know you love me. I'm willing to do whatever it takes to keep us together."

He didn't budge. "Like I said, I'm not ready for marriage."

"I know. You already said that." His words stung. I was aware of the facts. I didn't need to be reminded.

"Listen, Nina, I gotta go," he said nonchalantly. Then he hung up. I kept the receiver to my ear, the dial tone buzzing as I sat in disbelief. He had slipped through my fingers. This was different from whenever we'd broken up before because then it was in anger. This time Maurice was calm, almost too calm. He had thought out his decision, and unless I could come up with some sort of alternate solution, we were finished.

I hung up the phone. Becoming short of breath, I felt faint. I desperately wanted to call him back and beg him to reconsider. If I could only put the right combination of words together, maybe he would change his mind. But I knew Maurice, and calling would only add fuel to the fire, so instead I called Janelle and told her what happened.

"Good!" she said. "Now you should give that LJ Love a call. If you could run your fingers through his dreadlocks one good time, you'd forget about Maurice."

"This isn't funny, Janelle. I need your help."

"Nina, he wants out. What more does he need to say?"

Deep down I knew she was right, but that wasn't what I wanted to hear. Janelle wasn't giving me the kind of advice I was looking for, so I wanted to get off the phone as quickly as possible, but she wanted to keep talking.

"I'm not sure if I want to continue seeing Tim," she said.

"Uh-huh," I said. I was too much into my own pain to be a friend. I wanted to discuss me and my problem.

"We're really clicking, and I just want to be sure that my liking him isn't because I'm on the rebound and he came along at the right time."

"Uh-huh." Janelle got the picture and let me hang up, but first she made me promise not to call Maurice.

I broke my promise as soon as we hung up. Although I hadn't planned anything to say, I phoned to hear his voice and calm the sting in my heart. I wanted him to tell me that he'd spoken prematurely and that we wouldn't make any hasty decisions until we gave it more time.

I got his voice mail but couldn't bear to leave a message. I attempted to affirm myself the way that Janelle did when she and Corey broke up. "I can make it without Maurice," I said out loud. "I don't need him in my life. I will be just fine without him." But I didn't believe a word of it. I had just lost my man, and I didn't want to get over it. All the affirmations in the world weren't going to bring him back, so I stopped wasting my time and my breath.

I walked around my apartment in a daze. I sat at the kitchen table and picked up the newspaper to continue my job search, but I couldn't concentrate, so I got up again and paced. I found myself in the bathroom. I undressed and got into the shower and let the water fall on my face and my body. There was a burden on my shoulders that I couldn't remove, but I hoped the water would calm my spirit. I tilted my head back and allowed the water from the shower to join my tears. Frozen in the downpour, I didn't want to move, ever. I wasn't ready to start over again, meet someone new and get to know him. There was already a bond between Maurice and me, and I couldn't accept that it was broken.

In bed I lay awake for hours, going through our relationship from beginning to the end. It was worth fighting for, I told myself. I just didn't know what I would do. I kept hearing—and I know it was God—*Be patient. Don't do anything. Let time heal*—but I didn't want that answer. I fought with God for a while, but I became too tired to continue and eventually gave in to the advice, at least for the night.

A similiar dream. I was at a door and my parents were behind it.

"Smitty, no!" my mom yelled.

Again I could hear my dad throwing my mother around the room. "Please don't!" she cried.

I moved closer to the door and put my ear on it. I could hear my mother gurgling and gasping for air. He was strangling her. I fought to get the door open.

As the door opened my mom let out a horrifying scream. I ran through the door and fell. I found myself in a field of daisies having a picnic with Maurice. We were lying on a blanket, drinking wine and eating grapes. There was a gym across the field, and the ticket taker yelled, "Maurice, you're needed inside." Maurice looked at me and said, "I'll be right back." So I waited until it was dark. Then I stood up and walked toward the gym. As I got closer, I noticed Maurice coming out of the gym in his uniform, holding some girl's hand. They got into a car and drove away. Seeing them leave together was too painful, so I looked over my shoulder, and the field, the blanket, and everything on it were gone. I turned back around to see if Maurice was still in sight, but the stadium was gone. Before me were bars. I realized that I was in prison. I screamed to be let out. People walked by, but it was as if no one heard me.

The next morning I dragged myself out of bed and began a horrible workweek. I was ten minutes late two of the five days and just barely made it on time the other three. I couldn't stay focused. Completing daily tasks took more effort than I had to give. Maurice didn't call, and I became lethargic and depressed.

After work on Friday I put on my pajamas and stayed in them all weekend. My only distractions were watching old movies and eating. Every time the phone rang I checked my caller ID. None of the calls were from Maurice, so I didn't answer them.

.   .   .   .

A month went by without so much as a word from Maurice. I called him a few times, but I knew he had caller ID and assumed he was ignoring my calls. I would go to work and come straight home, unless it was necessary to stop. I refused to answer my phone. Some days I'd walk into the apartment and just lie and stare at the ceiling for hours, overwhelmed by pain. I'd tell myself to get over it, but the more I tried, the tougher it became. I scrutinized every move that I had made in the relationship and went over all the things that I could have done differently. I should have gone to Miami more. I should have been more understanding.

I felt that unless we were together, there would be no peace for me. But I couldn't make him love me. The thought of calling Leo crossed my mind, but I didn't want to waste his time. I knew he could never be what Maurice was to me.

Work was a chore. I desperately needed a change, something that would allow me to regain my sense of self-worth. This was one thing Janelle and I shared—we both had jobs we hated. She eventually used that common ground to lure me out of my bed to a job fair at the World Congress Center, which was close to my apartment. Knowing that the only way to reach me was in person, she came to my place on Saturday and nagged me until I got dressed and was ready to go.

"It's only a few blocks away. Why don't we walk?" Janelle suggested.

It was the middle of March, and although it was breezy, the sun warmed our faces as we walked down the sidewalk of the busy street.

"So, how are you holding up?" she asked.

"I'm not, really," I replied.

"You're going to be just fine."

"I guess I will be eventually," I said with a sigh. "I only wish I had your strength."

"You do, Nina. Trust me. Although I didn't want anyone to know, I was devastated when I broke up with Corey. I still care about him."

"I know you were hurt, Janelle," I said empathetically.

"Yes, but you'll never know how much. I cried myself to sleep many nights. I even thought about calling him on several occasions. It's been almost three months, and my fingers sometimes still begin dialing his number when I pick up the phone."

"But you have Tim," I said.

"Nina, Tim's nice. I like him a lot. He's actually proving to be a better catch. He's thoughtful, easygoing—he's even a member of my church."

"It's so large, who would know?"

"Exactly. He takes his profession seriously and is active in giving back to Atlanta as well as his hometown," she said proudly. "He's disciplined and conditions during the off season. And he isn't just out throwing money away. He's investing and planning for his children and theirs."

"That's good," I said dryly.

"*And* he takes the time to compliment me every time we go out. Even when he's busy, he never makes me feel like I'm a nuisance if I call at a bad time. As a matter of fact, he always seems pleased to hear from me."

"Uh-huh," I said, half listening. I was glad Tim was so great, but I wasn't exactly in the right frame of mind to hear her go on and on.

"I am going somewhere with all of this," she stated.

"Okay, then go already," I replied.

"I'm saying that when I needed a friend, Tim was there for me. He didn't push, he didn't expect anything more from me than a friendship. You know how sometimes it just feels good to be in the company of a man. Tim provided that for me."

"That's good, Janelle."

"There is someone who's dying to be a friend to you. Why won't you consider spending some time with Leo?"

"I thought about it," I said.

"Well, do it."

"Janelle, I love Maurice. Spending time with Leo would be using him."

"Not if you're up front with him about what you want."

"Maybe," I said. I had looked at his business card several times but could never bring myself to call. What would I say?

Maybe, I thought.

•　　•　　•　　•

The job fair turned out to be worthwhile. I set up two interviews, one with CNN Sports and the other with a local news station, KATL. Life is so unpredictable. I had to go to a job fair to get an interview with a company that I already had ties with. I was hopeful. I was determined to make the interviews count. Janelle wasn't excited about the pickings at the fair, but she also scored a few interviews, with small consulting firms.

That evening I called Cindy to get advice about my interviews.

"Hey, girl, it's so good to hear from you," Cindy said. "I've been so worried. You haven't called in a while."

"Yeah, well, Maurice and I broke up."

"I heard," she said, "but that doesn't mean we can't still be friends, right? Plus, I enjoy sharing my knowledge of the business with you. I think you're gonna do well, and I'd like to feel that I somehow had a hand in your success."

"Thank you, Cindy. You don't know how much it means to hear that from you."

"So, what's going on with you?" she asked.

"I landed two job interviews. One with CNN and one with KATL."

"Congratulations!"

"Can you give me some interview pointers?" I asked.

She told me exactly what I should wear, including hair and makeup. Then she quizzed me with a few questions that might be asked during the interviews. I was so grateful for her help. By the end of the conversation I felt confident and prepared.

"Thanks again," I said.

"Call me whenever you need to talk," she said.

"Okay."

"I mean it," she said. "Don't ever hesitate to call. Even if it's not business-related."

"Okay, Ms. High!"

"Plus, you gotta come visit me again. This time we'll skip the parties." We laughed. "We could go to the Bel Harbor Shops, and I could introduce you to some good contacts."

"That sounds good. Maybe."

"Just know that I'm here if ever you need anything," she said.

I hung up feeling good about having met Cindy. Even if Maurice and I didn't work out, I'd gotten a friend out of our roller-coaster relationship.

Two Steps Forward, One Step Back

Thirteen

I was thrilled to get the job at KATL. I would be a location reporter, going to sports bars and speaking with the locals about major games and other sports-related issues. The pay wasn't great, but I knew that with time and persistence I would prove myself and work my way up to sports anchor.

I immediately sent a thank-you note to Cindy. I knew she would be happy for me, and I used her own advice: "The best way to show gratitude is in writing." I couldn't wait to share the news with my parents, especially my father. But I kept it a secret until I went to their house for Sunday dinner.

I used my key to let myself in and walked through the living room. From the back door I saw an unusual sight: my mom and dad sitting together and talking outside on the deck. I could smell the smoke coming off the grill, and my mouth began to water. Mom had told me earlier over the phone that they would be grilling steaks, ribs, and salmon. I couldn't wait to chow down. And my parents' cookouts weren't complete without potato salad, coleslaw, green beans, baked beans, seven-layer salad, and freshly squeezed lemonade.

My mom jumped up when I tapped on the back door. "Nina, come on out," she said.

I joined them outside, and noticed that my dad's face was pale and blank.

"Hey, baby, how are you doing?" Mom said, and we hugged.

"Hey, Daddy," I said.

"Hi, Nina," he replied weakly. He looked like he was in a trance.

"You okay?" I asked.

"Fine, just fine," he replied. "So, how's Maurice? I caught the game last night, and he's definitely earning his pay."

"Daddy, we broke up!" I said irritably. Mom had said she'd told him about our breakup, and I couldn't believe how insensitive he was to even bring up Maurice's name.

"Oh, baby, I'm sorry," he said, the glazed look still in his eyes.

"Oh, don't mind your daddy," Mom interjected. "You know he's got a lot on his mind. Nina, come and taste the seven-layer salad, and wait till you see what I made for dessert."

She put her arm around my shoulder and led me toward the door. "Smitty, everything's going to be just fine," she said, and walked in behind me.

"What's going on, Momma?" I asked.

"Oh, nothing really. Your daddy and I were just having a talk."

"About what?"

"Well, Nina, it's personal stuff between us, nothing you need to worry about," she said, then added, "Trust me, everything is fine."

She was putting on her usual "pretend that our family has no problems" act. As much as I loved my mom, I envied Janelle's relationship with her mother—there was nothing they didn't talk about. My mom didn't even prepare me for the start of my menstrual cycle. I had to find out the hard way—coming home from school one day and finding blood in my underwear. Frightened that I was going to bleed to death, I laid several towels over my sheets, crawled into bed, and cried myself to sleep that night. Janelle's mom had prepped her ahead of time and even purchased a set of pads for her to practice with.

Then there were the serious issues of sex, drugs, and relationships. Juanita Lander always spoke about male-female relationships using quotes from her mother or some Bible verse. She'd say things like, "You gotta let a man be a man." And whenever I didn't clean my room, she'd walk by and say, "Nina, a man don't like an unkempt woman. He'll leave you in a heartbeat if you keep a dirty home." Her all-time favorite was Proverbs 31:10, "Who can find a virtuous woman? For her price is far above rubies."

There was never any heartfelt discussion. My mom never shared with me intimate things about her and Dad. Or about any other relationship she had before him. Growing up, it had never occurred to me that Mom could have possibly had a life before my dad. So I hadn't bothered asking. Not that I would have gotten an answer if I had.

Before long Brice and Brianna walked through the front door. "Hey, all!" Brice yelled as he rushed ahead of Brianna. "Oh, I smell the ribs a-grillin', and I can't wait to dig in!"

"Where's Brianna?" Mom asked.

"She's coming," he said, and walked back out onto the deck.

"Hey, Brianna! I'm sorry, but my son has no manners," Mom said when Brianna appeared in the kitchen. Brice came back in and wrapped his arm around Brianna. "I did my best with him," Mom teased, "but sometimes he forgets his good home training."

"Oh, it's okay," Brianna said in a timid voice. "He's just a bit excited."

"How are you?" I asked, looking directly into her eyes, searching for any sign that she feared Brice. There was actually a gleam in her eyes.

"Brianna, I was just giving Nina a taste of this seven-layer salad. Come and get a quick sample before dinner is served."

"Oooh, it looks good. What's in it?" she asked, and took a seat beside me at the kitchen table.

"Peas, bacon," Mom and I said, smiling when we realized we were talking at the same time.

"Go ahead," I said.

"Lettuce, mayo, cheese, celery, and onion. Plus a few secret seasonings." Mom put a sample in front of Brianna.

"Hey, bighead!" Brice said, swatting me on the back of the head.

"This is good," Brianna said.

"It's the best," I pronounced. Then I swung back and decked Brice in the chest, and he exaggerated his reaction to the blow. I turned away. "Brianna, how do you put up with him?" I asked.

"Brianna likes my playful side," he said, going behind her and tickling under her arms. It was obvious she was embarrassed, but she couldn't help but laugh.

"Say daddy," Brice teased. "Say big daddy!"

"Big daddy," she yelled, laughing.

"You're such a kid," she said, and punched him in the chest right where I'd punched him.

"Oh, two in a row!" he wailed, leaning over as if in agony. "You know you love me." He laughed. "All three of you love me because all women love B–R–I–C–E, because I'm just so sweet!"

"If you're so sweet, why is your breath so sour?" I wrinkled my nose, then reached for a high five from Brianna. She slapped my hand.

"Uh-oh, let me out of the kitchen," Brice moaned. "It's getting hot, and I feel a triple team coming on." Backing out, he yelled, "Hey, Dad, you need some help?" then made a quick getaway.

"I don't know how you put up with my son's craziness," Mom said to Brianna.

Brianna reciprocated with a strong, sincere stare. "Because I love him, Mrs. Lander."

. . . .

We ate dinner out on the deck. It was a bit nippy, but the spring weather was coming early. The sun was out and the breeze was nice. My dad turned on the outdoor heater as the sun began to set, while Mom and I brought dessert from the kitchen. It was one of my favorites, key lime pie and ice cream. Once the pie was served I decided it was time to share my news.

"I have an announcement to make," I said.

"So do I," Brice interrupted. "But I'm going to prove that I have manners. You can go first."

I rolled my eyes at him and began, "Dad, Mom, I'm pleased to report that your baby girl and most beautiful of your two children has landed a sports-reporting job with KATL."

"That's great, Nina," Mom asked, excited. "When do you start?"

"Well, it's about time you got a real job," my dad said. I was crushed. I'd thought he would be proud of me. "Will you be making a decent salary?"

I refused to answer. It wasn't his business as far as I was concerned.

"Now, Smitty, you know that reporters have to prove themselves before they get a competitive salary."

"So what you gonna be reporting?" he asked.

"Sports," I answered dryly, feeling deflated.

"Well, that's what you wanted, right?" Brice asked.

"Yeah, that's what I wanted," I managed.

"Well, good," Dad said. "Do a good job so you can get your salary increased. You know that you have to work harder than anybody in that station because you got two things going against you: you're black and you're a woman. It's gonna be hard."

I waited for some words of encouragement, but my dad wasn't much for that. If Brice had said it, my father would jump on the bandwagon, but with me it was different. I would have to prove that I could be successful in my chosen field before he would believe in me.

"Congrats, Nina," Brianna offered.

"Thank you."

"I can't wait to see you on TV, Ninu," Brice chimed in. "I'll make sure everyone at the spa watches."

"Thank you, Brice." He surprised me by not throwing in any jokes.

"Now it's time for my news," Brice said, rising to his feet. "Mom, Dad, Nina . . . stand up with me, Brianna." She stood and he put his arm around her. "Everybody, Brianna and I are engaged, and we're planning to marry in five months, in August."

"What? Brice, Brianna! Oh, good! Good!" Mom said, overjoyed.

"Congratulations, son," Dad said.

Was I the only one who saw this as a great mistake? Granted, they wanted to get married, but why rush? They were in love now, but when the infatuation wore off, Brice would probably treat Brianna like Dad treats Mom. He would dominate her and try to control her life. And since when did Brice ever commit to one woman? This was a disaster waiting to happen.

I looked up, and while Mom hugged Brianna and Brice hugged Dad, Brianna saw my face. I was caught.

Fourteen

The TV station put me through a two-week orientation, and by the time I was in front of the camera I was anxious but more than ready to show off my abilities to the greater Atlanta metropolis. After all, I had been training for this job since I watched the L.A. Lakers beat the Philadelphia 76ers 109–102 in the 1980 NBA Championship. That was a magical season—the three-point field goal and rookies Earvin Johnson and Larry Bird were amazing. From then on I was hooked on sports—especially basketball. I loved hearing people's opinions about players and teams and statistics and even began forming my own, paying careful detail to predicting championship players and teams.

My first assignment was the lunch crowd at the Varsity Sports Bar. It was me, my cameraman, Gus, who had been with the station for some time and wasn't happy that he was assigned to a rookie, and the rowdy patrons, who were overly enthusiastic about sharing their comments on the evening's Atlanta-Chicago game. I rode over in one of the station's vans with Gus, who only spoke to me when I spoke to him. When we arrived at the location he just sat in the van.

"Are you coming in?" I asked.

"I'll be there in a minute," he replied nonchalantly. I jumped out and walked into the bar to scout locations for the shoot and find groups of people who seemed to be interested in any of the bar's many sports screens. By the time he came in holding his camera, I had my plan organized and my interviewees prepped. He saw me but didn't walk over. I swallowed my pride and approached him.

"I was thinking that we could go into the room in the back. There seems to be a lively bunch in there."

"Whatever," he said, and scratched his bulging stomach.

He followed me into the room. I looked to him for a cue to begin, but he stood back, probably testing my competence.

I said, "Gus, I'd like to begin my introduction with this group of people around me. They've already been prepped. Then we'll float around through the bar to interview individuals I've chosen."

He shrugged.

I got the group to surround me and told them when the red light on the camera came on to yell, "Go, Hawks!"

After they did their part I introduced the segment. "Hello, all you Hawks fans! This is Nina Lander reporting from the Varsity Sports Bar and Grill. I'm here this afternoon with a group of rowdy fans who are hoping for a win against the Chicago Bulls. Since the retirement of Michael Jordan last year, the Hawks are sure to land a victory this evening!"

The crowd behind me yelled and screamed to show their support. Gus didn't say a word. "Okay, Gus, if you think that intro was okay, we can start the individual interviews."

"Uh–huh," he said, and followed me. We made our way through the bar and got good responses from the interviewees. I had an eye for true fans. I knew sports, and I knew what questions to ask. To end the segment we found another rowdy group to share closing words.

"I think that'll be enough for the segment," I said to Gus. "Do you have any additional suggestions?"

"Nope," he said.

I cringed. How could he be so indifferent and unhelpful? He was stuck with me, and we needed to make the best of the situation. I kept my composure and made my way to the van. Gus took his time and loaded the camera in the back of the van, then walked around, opened his door, and got in the driver's seat. We pulled out of the lot and rode back to the station in silence.

Once we parked in the station's lot, Gus reached for the door, then looked back at me. "Not bad, rookie," he said. Then he got out of the van, and slammed his door.

"Thank you," I said with a slight grin. I was satisfied. And although I knew Gus wasn't thrilled to be working with a newcomer, he had to respect my abilities.

.   .   .   .

When I got home from work, I was really feeling good about myself, so I decided to cook a nice gourmet meal and invite Janelle over to celebrate with me. Unfortunately, when I called she was on her way to meet Tim for dinner, and suggested we get together later in the week. I put a hip-hop CD on the stereo and began to dance around. I sashayed my way into my bedroom. Before I knew it, I was jumping up and down, dancing on the bed.

The phone rang, and I fell back on the bed out of breath and reached over and picked up.

"I feel guilty. Are you okay?" It was Janelle calling from her mobile.

"I'm fine," I said.

"You sure? I can cancel with Tim, if you want me to."

"Thank you, Anna Mae, but I'm having a solo party, and trust me, all is well."

She laughed. "Okay, but I'll have my cell on, so call me if you need anything."

"Yes, ma'am. Love you!"

"I love you too, Nina. And Nina . . ."

"Huh?"

"Why don't you call Leo?"

"Girl, stop feeling sorry for me. I told you I was okay."

"Okay, okay! It was just a suggestion."

"Bye!" I said.

"Bye!"

I hung up and lay back on my pillow. I remembered the first time I met Maurice. I believed it was fate that we met. And although we hadn't spoken in some time, I knew there was no way we were over. I felt it in my bones. My good friend heartache began to creep back, but I wasn't going to entertain it, at least not at that moment. Things had been going too well.

I recapped the events of the day to myself, and my smile returned. I was energized and wanted to escalate the feeling. Maybe I should call Leo. I decided I had nothing to lose, so I jumped off the bed and went to my closet to look for the purse I'd carried to the New Year's party. I found it buried underneath the numerous baseball caps that I owned but seldom wore. When I opened it, there was his card. I read over it several times, then looked on the back. Leo had written his home number and "Call me if you ever need to talk."

"Whoa," I said aloud. My heart was thumping through my chest. "I can't do this!"

I threw the card on the bed and turned the music down. Attempting to distract myself from the task at hand, I opened the refrigerator and began pulling out ingredients for dinner. But Leo's message was whispering to me: "Call me if you ever need to talk."

I tried to ignore it but couldn't. I ran back upstairs, picked up the card, and brought it back down with me. I walked over to the sofa and stared at the message. "I can do this!" I declared.

Finally, I took a deep breath and dialed his number. He won't be there, I assured myself. He's busy. I'll just hang up when I get the answering machine.

The phone rang twice.

"Hello," said the voice on the other end. I paused, waiting to hear the rest of the message, but there was silence.

"Hello," he said again.

I had to answer. "Hello."

"Who is this?" he said, raising his voice a bit.

"Leo?" I asked.

"Who wants to know?" he asked defensively. I was embarrassed and nearly hung up the phone.

"Who is this?" he asked.

"It's Nina. Is this Leo?"

"Nina. Nina Lander," he said with excitement in his voice.

"Yeah."

"Hold on," he said. I took another deep breath and tapped my fingers against the receiver until he was back on the line.

"Sorry about that," he said. "I was on the phone with my manager."

"Oh, do you need me to call you back?" I asked apologetically.

"No. I have Nina Lander on the telephone. Nothing else is more important than this moment right here. So, how are you?"

"I'm good."

"I saw you on TV today. Congrats."

"You saw me?" I was surprised.

"Yeah, all of Atlanta saw. You were great. Now I'm going to have my TV tuned to KATL every day at four and again for the repeat at eleven to see Miss Nina Lander reporting on sports."

"You're too much!" I said. We shared a nervous laugh.

"So, how may I help you, mademoiselle?" he asked.

"Well, I didn't want anything in particular. I just called to say hello and I guess to talk."

"I'm all ears," he said.

"I don't have anything planned or set to say."

"Well, you don't have to. We can talk about anything and everything, or nothing at all." I liked his voice. I didn't know much about him, but I was intrigued.

"So, how long have you been back in Atlanta?" I asked.

"Not even a year, but I'm gonna make this my home again."

"I am too." I said. "I love Atlanta. So, do you have a girlfriend here?"

"No, I don't. I'm extremely single." He chuckled. So did I.

"What do you do for fun, when you're not doing the rap thing?" I asked.

"I hang out with my friends, play piano, sax, drums, and a few other instruments."

"I don't remember you being in the school band."

"I wasn't!"

"Okay! So what other hidden talents do you have?"

"I wouldn't call it a talent, but I am multilingual," he said.

"Really?" I hadn't expected that.

"Yeah. I speak French, Spanish, and two African languages fluently. And I dabble in a few others." Then he told me my eyes were as beautiful as a starlight night in each language.

"I'm impressed."

"There's more where that came from," he said.

Charming, I thought. Before I knew it I was rolling out questions as if I were interviewing him for a show, but he didn't seem to mind. Leo was patient and seemed to answer every question candidly. He had a quirky sense of humor, but it worked for him.

Back in elementary school, Leo had lived with his grandparents during the school year, but in the summer, while the rest of his classmates were away at camp or hanging around, he and his mom traveled around the world. She was something of a modern-day gypsy and had friends throughout the world. Because he and his mother spent months at a time in places like Ghana, Paris, Rome, and Spain, Leo was very open-minded and familiar with many cultures. Whenever his mom was traveling in the States during the holidays, he traveled with her.

I asked Leo, "So how did your mom manage to pay for the travel and lodging?"

"She's amazing," he said. "You really should meet her one day. She worked to get airfare whenever we were out of the country. We'd live with a variety of entertainment types. Plus, she sang and danced, sometime as an exotic dancer, to see the world."

"Wow, your childhood must have been interesting."

"In more ways than I can share with you in one conversation. Maybe that's why I wasn't one of the most popular guys in school. I was bored with the things that excited most high school students and didn't care about being the most popular brother in school. I had other things on my mind, one being how my mom was doing out there in the world without me."

"I'm sure. Where was your dad during all of this?"

"Well, I was conceived during a one-night stand," he said, laughing.

"Oh."

"No, really, and I don't have a problem with it. I respect my mother's lifestyle, and, well, I guess I'm a product of it. But I do know that my dad is a musician. I'm sure he's out there doing exactly what I do—entertaining.

"You're so fascinating," I said.

"Not really," he said. "Well, maybe I am. But right now I'd like to know more about you."

"There's not much to tell," I said.

"Well, I do know a few things about you. I know that your birthday is September fifteenth."

"Right," I answered, not revealing my surprise that he knew this. "And when's yours?"

"January twenty-first, but we're talking about you right now. I know you love old movies, seafood, your favorite season is autumn, and you absolutely hate it when men are rude to women. I could go on."

"How do you know these thing about me?"

"I'm observant, and I've always had a way of finding out about things I need to know."

It was easy to talk to Leo about myself. I shared my plan to become one of the most notable anchors around, and talked about my time in college. He was an attentive listener, commenting at all the right places. He made me feel so relaxed that I wanted to pour out my heart and tell him what I felt for Maurice. Or talk about my concerns about my parents' relationship and Brice's engagement to Brianna, but the conversation was going too well and I didn't want to bring up anything that would change the flow.

When the conversation began to wind down, he said, "I look forward to talking to you again, soon."

"So do I," I said. "This has been nice."

I hung up feeling smitten. I could get used to being in the company of such an interesting and respectful man.

Fifteen

Leo and I quickly grew close. I found myself looking forward to speaking with him over the phone several times a day. I'd call him on breaks and tell him how my day was going, and he'd call me in the evenings just before he went to sleep. Sometimes we'd talk for hours, even when I had to be up early for work, but I was so excited about my job that my energy seemed endless. After a few weeks we finally scheduled a time to get together. Leo suggested an offbeat coffee shop located in Little Five Points. He gave me directions, and we met on a Sunday afternoon.

I dressed in a long peach sundress, a spring hat, and dark shades. I wanted to appear mysterious and have the opportunity to really check him out without his knowing. I arrived a few minutes early, ordered a latte, and took a seat at a table with a window view. Before long a dreaded god walked through the door. The first thing I noticed about Leo was his open-toe sandals, which were trendy and fit his look so well. He wore wide-leg khakis and a loose, earth-toned tunic. As I took in all that was Leo, I was drawn to his beautiful green eyes, which I had never noticed before, and his shoulder-length dreadlocks. He had this Lenny Kravitz, Terence Trent D'Arby, Eric Benet thing going on, with a hip-hop flavor. His whole image was unique and quite appealing.

As he approached me, I removed my shades. "Hi!"

"Nina Lander, in the flesh," he said, and walked over to me with his arms spread. I got up from my seat and fell into his embrace. Nice.

"I got here a little early, so I went ahead and ordered."

"That's cool," he said. "Do you want anything else? They have some good pastries and whatnots up there."

"I'm fine."

"How about I bring you a dessert, and if you like it, cool. If not, you don't have to eat it."

"Okay," I replied.

"Why don't you sit back down and I'll be back before you know it," he said, and I watched him walk over to the counter.

I knew I had to be careful spending time with him because he was everything a woman would want in a man. And I knew I wasn't that woman because my heart belonged to someone else.

Leo returned to the table with a coffee for himself and two scrumptious-looking pastries.

"This is a La Torta di Mezzanotte," he said, pushing the plate in front of me. "Try it. I think you'll like it. It reminds me of the treats my mom would bring me in Europe when she'd come in after a party."

I smiled and took a bite of the rich chocolate torte. "Yum," I said.

"You like it! Some girls I date are scared to experiment and try new things, you know?"

"I guess."

"Well, I know this isn't a date, but you know what I mean," he said apologetically.

"Of course," I replied.

We sipped our hot drinks and settled into a nice silence. Leo seemed comfortable, and so was I until we managed to look up simultaneously and catch each other's eyes. I quickly looked away.

"You're not nervous, are you?" he asked.

"No. It just feels weird. I haven't seen you since high school, and even then I didn't know you all that well. So I have this weird feeling that I've known you for years, but then I don't really know you at all."

"So, what do you want to know?" he asked.

"I look at your background and your different interests and your range of talents, and I can't help but wonder why you chose to become a rapper."

"For one, I like rapping. I enjoy the art form. Plus it pays well."

"Some wouldn't consider it an art form," I replied, probing for a deeper answer.

"Well, that's only because it was created by members of a supposed sub-American culture."

"Go on."

"Seriously, hip-hop culture has gained international acceptance. It's made a tremendous impact on world history, especially U.S. history. I wanted to be part of the phenomenon."

"I can understand that, but it seems to me that you'd be more at home in an orchestra or something," I said.

He laughed. "Do I look like the type that would blend well in a symphony orchestra?"

"I guess not." I laughed along with him.

"My mom was disappointed at first, but now she has mad respect for my chosen profession." He leaned in closer. "Nina, it makes me proud that people around the world are moved by my music and the messages in my lyrics."

"I'm sure it's overwhelming at times."

"Yeah, it can be, but I realize the responsibility that comes with the talent the Creator has blessed me with, and I know it's my duty to be true to that."

I liked his style. He was confident, intelligent, well-traveled, but with roughneck tendencies. I was enjoying life through Leo's eyes, but I knew something had to be wrong with him. If he was such a good catch, why was he still single?

"So . . ." I eased into my question. "Why haven't you gotten married?"

"I've been waiting for you," he said, flashing an irresistible smile, and then put a piece of torte in his mouth.

I didn't want to hear any lines from him. I just wanted us to be straightforward with each other and talk as man and woman.

"Sorry," he said. "I'm sure that's probably too difficult to believe, so I'll give you the standard answer that I use when any other woman asks that question."

"Leo, I don't feel like playing games," I said.

"I understand, and trust me, that's not my way." He paused briefly. "I'm still young, plus I haven't found my soul mate yet. I refuse to surrender to anyone but the lady who was predestined with the key to my heart."

"That's sweet."

"It's true. So, what about you, Nina? Are you going to marry the brother you're with now?" He watched me closely.

"We broke up," I said hesitantly. I hadn't planned to tell him anything about me and Maurice, but since he'd asked I figured I'd come clean, while sharing details sparingly.

"I'd be lying if I said I wasn't glad to hear that," he said. "But I'm sure that's not the correct response."

"No, it's not."

"I saw the way he reacted after I walked away from you at the New Year's Eve party. I hope I didn't cause any static."

"No, you didn't," I lied.

"So, are you okay with the breakup?" he asked.

"I'm fine."

"Is it what you wanted?"

"No, Leo, it isn't what I wanted. To be honest, I'm still in love with him." I just blurted it out; I hadn't meant to be that blunt. I sat back in my chair to watch his reaction. I was sure our rendezvous would end after that.

"I can respect that," he said calmly. I could tell that he didn't want to know too much more.

"Leo, you wrote on the back of your card for me to call if I ever needed to talk."

"And I meant that," he said.

"Well, I need to talk from time to time, but I'm not ready to move into another relationship. I'm still hoping things will work out for me and Maurice."

"So that's his name. Maurice?"

"Yeah."

"Does he live here in Atlanta?"

"No, he lives in Miami."

"Oh." He leaned back in his chair and took a breath. "Well, let's do this. Why don't we not mention Maurice's name, unless you really need to talk about him. Otherwise, let's continue to enjoy each other's company whenever it works out, with no strings attached."

"Okay," I said, amazed at his cool, laid-back nature.

"I just want you to understand that I've had a crush on you since our freshman year in high school. The first time I saw you was in the gym helping to decorate for the first dance of the year. I know you didn't notice me, but I was helping the deejay set up."

"No, I'm sorry, but I didn't," I said, wondering where he was going with this.

"My point is, if we're going to be friends, let's just be friends. I won't go any further than you let me."

"I would hope not," I said.

"I am a man, all man, but I'm also human," he said. "Keep that in mind."

"What are you trying to say?" I asked.

"I've come to learn that sometimes people do things without thinking about the consequences, or how it will affect the other person. I want us to always be honest with each other about our feelings and actions. We'll always be good friends as long as we can do that."

"In that case," I said, "I think we're destined to have a positive and flourishing friendship."

.   .   .   .

Leo invited me to numerous outings with him and his many friends, and other times we'd hang out with Janelle and Tim. I had a small niche of friends: Janelle and my college sorors, but Leo didn't hang with one group or type. He was cool with the other entertainers in Atlanta and was always invited to their private functions. But there were also his Jamaican friends, Hispanic friends, African spiritualists, and his old deejay chums from high school. He floated in and out of each circle with ease.

Spending time with him always meant some new and different experience for me. I even liked hanging out in the studio while he worked on his new album. I met his mother on a few occasions, and she was quite fascinating: opinionated, blunt, open, and extremely spiritual, quite a free thinker. Her stories about her travels were captivating. She was crazy about Leo.

Once, when the three of us were hanging out and Leo had to leave the room to answer his cell phone, she said to me, "I know you two are just friends, and I'm glad of that. Friendship is the basis of any worthwhile relationship."

"You're right," I replied.

"Now I'm going to tell you something. My son is a good man—the best!"

Was she trying to sell her son to me?

"And because he's the best," she continued, "I want the best for him."

"I'm sure you do, Ms. Jones."

"Now, I know my boy knows how to take care of himself. He's proven that to me over and again. But I know how fond he is of you, and I just want to make sure you're aware of it."

"I think I know," I said.

"But you feel differently, right?"

"Well . . ." I wasn't sure how to answer.

"I would never tell you what to do because you are not my child, but I like you, so I'm going to share some advice with you, woman to woman."

"Okay." I swallowed.

"If your heart is not in it, don't allow yourself to get too close, because when certain lines are crossed and the emotions aren't reciprocated, things have a tendency to become complicated. And that wouldn't be fair to my son, of course, but it wouldn't be fair to you either."

"Yes, ma'am," I replied.

"And life, my dear, brings with it enough dips and curves without us adding to them," she said with a smile.

Message received.

Sixteen

Between establishing myself as a sports reporter and spending time with Leo, I was so busy that spring flew by. With the end of spring came the end of basketball season, the beginning of baseball season, and the push to finalize the plans for Brice's wedding. It was a time of change. I could feel it in my bones, and the evidence was beginning to mount.

Janelle finally quit her job and registered for a full-time load of summer classes at Emory Business School. Tim was busy with baseball. The bond between Leo and me was stronger than ever, but with him preparing for his upcoming tour and me working longer hours and filling in for other reporters, we were spending less time together.

I was so eager to prove myself to the station that in addition to my location sports stories, I'd report on just about anything that seemed newsworthy. To deliver an effective story, I'd stand in the middle of pouring rain during a dreaded Atlanta tornado and pray I wouldn't be harmed. As my contacts expanded, I'd get tips on numerous newsworthy occurrences in the city and go chasing after them with all the gusto I could muster. Gus and I would race across town to the scene of a crime or an accident to be the first to get the scoop.

Most evenings when I finally got in after a long day I'd be too tired to talk to Leo on the phone and unwilling to invite him over too late. I didn't want to be tempted to cross the line his mother had warned me about. Many nights I'd want company and need to feel a man close to me, but I'd resist.

One Saturday night Leo called after a late rehearsal. I had just walked in the door and was glad to hear his voice. I hadn't seen him in several days, and I missed him.

"So, how was your day?" he asked.

"Too long."

"You feel like meeting me at the coffee shop?" he asked.

"Oh, Leo, I'm too tired."

"That's cool," he said. He already knew not to ask to come to my place after a certain time—it had been agreed upon in the early stages of our relationship.

"I miss you," I said, feeling guilty for turning him down.

"Yeah, I miss you too," he replied in a dull tone. "Well, I'm about to leave the studio and head back to my place."

The strangest feeling came over me. I didn't want him to go back to his place. I wanted him to come here and spend the night with me. I really cared about him, and I was beginning to give up on the idea of Maurice and I getting back together. I rationalized that if Leo came over this late, it'd be no big deal, we'd just spend some time talking and eventually fall asleep. I needed to fall asleep in someone's arms for a change, and if we did make love, well, we cared about each other, and that was reason enough.

"Hey, why don't you come over here?" I suggested.

"But we agreed—" he began.

"I know what we said, but I really want to see you and I'm too tired to come out. You can just stay the night."

"I don't know, Nina," he said.

"Just come," I insisted. There was a long silence.

"Okay, I'm on my way," he said. He sounded uneasy, but he was coming over and I knew we'd both feel more comfortable once he got here.

I took a quick shower and slipped on a T-shirt and shorts. I didn't want to have on anything that was too sexy or revealing. It was important that he didn't get the wrong idea. I quickly tidied up and rummaged through my videos to see if there was something we'd both enjoy watching.

But I was fooling myself—I knew deep down what I was planning. And I wanted to convince myself and him that it would be a mere coincidence. That making love that evening couldn't have possibly been premeditated.

Between the time we hung up the phone and when Leo finally buzzed from downstairs, I didn't sit still once. My heart raced and my palms were sweaty. I was afraid to open the door. I knew if we did make love, there would be no turning back.

He walked in, his awesome presence filling the room. I inhaled deeply but didn't release my breath. We hugged. I breathed deeply, to absorb the energy that flowed between us.

"I've missed you," he whispered, then slowly released me.

"Me too." I decided to change the subject. "I chose a couple movies from my limited collection."

"Oh, okay," he said. "So what ya got?"

"*Pillow Talk* and *The Seven Year Itch*," I said as we walked over to the sofa.

"Let's watch whatever you haven't seen," he suggested.

"I've seen them both," I replied.

"So have I. Which is your favorite? You choose."

He sat down and began removing his shoes while I put a tape in the VCR. I grabbed the remote control and slowly walked toward him. I had two choices: to take a seat on the opposite end of the sofa or to snuggle close to him. I decided to pace myself in case I changed my mind, or made up my mind. I wasn't quite sure which side of the coin I had chosen.

The trailers began. "Do you want me to fast-forward through these?" I asked.

"If you want to." He seemed a little edgy.

"How about I let them run and you can tell me how rehearsal went," I said.

"It went well. The first performance of the tour is going to be here in Atlanta at the Atrium."

"Good. I can't wait to see you perform live."

"Yeah?" he asked shyly.

"Yeah. It was exciting to watch you at work in the studio, but I bet you're off-the-hook onstage."

"I can't wait to begin touring. There's so much more involved with the stage performance. The energy is unbeatable. You'll see."

"So, when is the performance here?"

"In two weeks!"

"That soon?"

"Yeah, that soon, but believe me, I will be ready. This is what I was born to do."

We both smiled. Then there was silence as we watched the final trailer. When the opening credits for the movie began I felt Leo's eyes on me. I returned his gaze.

"You don't have to sit so far away," he said. "You can move closer. It feels funny having you way on the other end of the couch."

It was true: it didn't feel right. I inched over to him. But the closer I got, the more turned-on I became.

The movie began and we watched, but neither of us was paying attention. I was doomed from the start. For one, we both had already seen the movie. Two, it wasn't my favorite. I just chose something I thought he'd like. I made every attempt to get involved in it, but my hormones were getting the best of me.

"Do you want some popcorn?" I asked.

"No, I'm cool."

"Do you mind if I get comfortable?" I asked.

"As a matter of fact . . ." He rearranged himself into a lounging position with one leg hanging off the sofa. I sat between his legs and rested my head on his chest.

"That's much better," he said. "Are you comfortable?"

"Yeah, this feels good."

I attempted to watch the movie, but I couldn't. I was bored and restless, but I was also tired. I eventually drifted off to sleep.

I was awakened by Leo nudging me. There was static on the television. "Did I fall asleep?" I asked.

"We both did," he said. "Let's get in bed. Is that okay?"

"Okay," I said and we walked to my room.

"Do you mind if I take off my pants?" he asked.

"No, go ahead. I want you to be comfortable."

He sat at the edge of the bed and removed his pants and his shirt. I pulled back the covers, and we got in. Him on his side and me on mine. Soon we gravitated close to each other and fell off to sleep.

·   ·   ·   ·

I don't remember dreaming or when I fell asleep, but when I awoke and looked over at the clock it was 6:30 A.M., too early to get up on a Sunday. When I stretched and my foot rubbed against Leo's leg, I knew there was no way I was getting back to sleep.

I looked over at him, and the streetlights shining into the loft were like a dim spotlight on his face. Although he was a handsome man, I saw right through his looks and thought about all his wonderful qualities. He was the kind of man that you'd commit to with confidence, knowing he'd treat you like a lady and put forth effort to maintain the relationship.

I reached over and stroked his face, then moved closer to him. He rolled over on his side, put his arms around me, and began to rub my back.

He was awake, I thought. Who could sleep with all the sexual energy that was in the air?

He opened his eyes, and before I knew it a boldness overcame me and I kissed him. He kissed back. It was warm, sensual, meaningful. My mind was screaming, Stop, before you go too far. But the rest of me demanded exactly what was happening between Leo and me.

Leo lifted my T-shirt over my head. When I looked up he was gazing into my eyes. We smiled. He tenderly caressed my breast as we kissed again. I reached to help him remove his boxers, but he slowly moved his hand over mine to stop me.

"Are you sure you want to do this?" he asked.

I nodded. "Yeah. What about you?"

"I know what I want," he replied. "I just want to make sure you do too."

He looked at me intently, then began to kiss my neck, my shoulders.

The passion that I felt was overwhelming. I knew he was as into this as I was. As we kissed, our tongues performed a rhythmic dance, and I knew that being with him like this meant much more than just having sex.

For the first time since my first time, I felt like I was actually consummating a relationship. When we joined in a sexual union, I felt a combination of pleasure and spiritual oneness. It was the strangest and one of the most fulfilling experiences I'd ever had with a man. It felt so good that I became frightened. I had crossed the line, but I wasn't sure if I was ready to accept the responsibility of doing so. Leo was a man in every sense of the word. Either we were to move forward as a couple or we would remain friends. There was no in-between for him. I froze.

"Are you okay?" he asked.

I couldn't answer.

"Does it not feel good to you?"

"No, that's not it at all," I replied. "It feels too good."

"It's supposed to, right?"

"Right," I said, smiling. Leo moved his lips over mine. I pushed aside all apprehension and met him at his level of passion, falling into the deepest place of ecstasy that I'd ever been.

Seventeen

We slept late and were awakened by the phone.

"Hey, Nina," Brianna said when I answered.

"Hey." I was groggy.

"I'm just calling to remind you of our brunch date at one-thirty."

"Am I late?" I asked.

"No, you have an hour. I just wanted to make sure you didn't forget. Did you?"

"No, I didn't forget," I lied.

"Okay. So I'll see you in about an hour at La Madeline in Buckhead, off of West Paces Ferry."

"All right, see you then," I mumbled, and hung up the phone.

I turned over to Leo. He rested his face in his hand.

"I'm sorry," I said. "I forgot I was supposed to meet Brianna to discuss my role in the wedding. She asked me to be her maid of honor. I'm going to have to throw her a shower and do all the other things a maid of honor does."

"No problem," he said.

I reached over and snuggled my nose into his cheek, then lightly kissed it. "I need to move quickly."

We got out of bed, and Leo began searching under the covers for his boxers. First he pulled out my bikini panties and passed them to me with an embarrassed look on his face. He seemed amused when he finally found his underwear at the foot of the bed.

I took a shower, and when I got out Leo was fully dressed, shoes and all, and downstairs listening to his new CD. "I forgot to give you this last night," he said.

"Oh, wow! That sounds great. Thank you." I closed my eyes, snapped my fingers, and began moving to Leo's alternative-rap sound. His style was a mixture of Arrested Development and the Fugees, with a hint of Outkast. Leo joined me in my dance.

"I'll listen to this on my way to meet Brianna," I said.

"Good. Maybe you'll think about me."

"And you know that," I said, and kissed him.

"Let's get out of here," he said. "I have to go home and get dressed. I'm supposed to be shopping with someone from A&R to get some ideas for my stage look."

"Okay." I grabbed my purse and keys, and we headed out. We gave each other quick kisses good-bye and hugged before we went our separate ways. I felt good about having made love with Leo. From the feeling of his embrace, so did he.

．　　　．　　　．　　　．

I arrived at the restaurant about ten minutes late. Brianna sat sipping a soda. I took a seat across from her and started apologizing.

"Don't worry about it," she insisted. "I'm just glad you made it, and I'm glad you're going to be my maid of honor."

"Well, what can I say." Literally. How could I have said no? My family would have disowned me.

Brianna had her bridal-planning book out and was leafing through the pages. She seemed flustered.

"So, are you on schedule with your planning, or are we going to have to do some crunching?" I asked.

"Well, my mother has been so overbearing. She wants to take over the planning, and we have two totally different visions. My stepdad has tried to calm her down, but you would think she was planning for her own wedding."

I nodded and listened.

"My two sisters live in different states. One's in Chicago and the other's in Philly. Neither will be here until the week before the wedding. My best friend got a job offer in New York, of all places, at the beginning of the year and isn't here to help me." She sighed. "All I have are a few people from the spa who I've gotten to know, and this girl from my job, but I don't know about her—she seems more interested in seeing how things are going to turn out than in being helpful."

As Brianna explained what she'd worked out with her mother and told me about the people at her job wanting to give her a separate shower, I realized that I knew absolutely nothing about her, her family—I didn't even know what she did for a living. I had a lot of catching up to do, and I really wasn't up for the job.

She must have noticed that I wasn't keeping pace because she stopped midsentence. "I'm so sorry for going on and on. I'm just a bit stressed, and, well, I know I need to just calm down, but this is a lot." Her eyes widened as she stared directly into mine. I could sympathize.

The waitress walked up and asked if she could take our order.

"Oh, we're not ready," Brianna said. "I'm sorry. Do you know what you want, Nina?"

"I'm sure I can decide now," I said, hoping to get out as quickly as possible. I scanned the menu. "I'll have a tuna salad sandwich and a bottled water."

"I'll have a chicken Caesar salad," Brianna said.

The waitress gathered our menus and walked away.

Brianna's expression changed from frustrated to worried. Then she took a deep breath and asked, "How have you been?"

"Oh, I've been fine. Why do you ask?"

"I feel funny telling you this, and maybe I shouldn't, but if I were you, I'd want to know, so I'm going to tell you." She spoke in a low voice, as if she was worried someone in the restaurant was eavesdropping on our conversation.

"What is it?" I asked.

"Well, I was at the spa yesterday, and Maurice was in there getting a manicure and pedicure."

"Oh really."

"Well, yeah. And he told Brice that he'd moved here for the summer."

"What?" I couldn't believe my ears. Was she playing a trick on me, or trying to get me back because she knew I wasn't enthused about her and my brother getting married. But why would she do that?

"I'm sorry," she said, and winced. "I shouldn't have said anything, but I was as surprised as you are now, and I wanted you to know before you ran into him at the spa or something. I remember New Year's, and I know from Brice that you still care about him, and, well, I just thought you should know."

I wasn't prepared for that kind of news. Not then, and not coming from her. And especially not after I had made love to Leo that morning. Maurice being in Atlanta could mean a lot of things. Having the opportunity to talk about what went wrong with our relationship. Getting back together. Hurting Leo, who I cared deeply for. How could I sit here another minute, knowing this? I wanted to get up out of my seat, get in my car, and go home to think.

"Are you okay?" Brianna asked.

I came to. "Wow! That's some news."

"I hope I wasn't out of line."

"No. Thank you. I needed to know, and you're right, it's better that I hear it this way than end up bumping into him somewhere without warning."

I tapped my fingers on the table, stared off across the restaurant, and wondered how soon we could finish brunch. The waitress brought our meals and my water, but now I wasn't hungry.

We spent about an hour going through all the details of the reception that Brianna had not yet attended to, which was pretty much everything except for booking the place. She had the church scheduled and the minister chosen but hadn't planned the entertainment or the ceremony. She had already chosen her dress, her color scheme, and the dress patterns and tuxedo ensembles for the wedding party.

She was nearly in tears when we realized everything that hadn't been done.

"My mother and I have been doing so much bickering, and my job is so demanding, that I didn't realize I was this far behind. I'm usually an organized person."

"What do you do?" I finally asked.

"I'm a legal secretary."

"Do you have any personal time?"

"I'm taking my personal time and vacation time to cover being off two weeks before the wedding, a week for the honeymoon, and a week to begin decorating the house."

"You're remodeling. Good," I said, pleased that my brother's bachelor pad would finally have a woman's touch.

"No. Brice didn't tell you? We're moving into a bigger house."

I'd had no idea. Why was I the last to know everything that went on with my family? But I chose not to overreact. I was supposed to be here for Brianna, not the other way around.

"If you can't get time off, why don't you get a coordinator?" I suggested. "It would make things so much easier."

"I didn't think I'd be able to get one at this late date, especially for a reasonable price," she replied frantically.

"I'll tell you what. Janelle has a family friend who's a wedding coordinator. I hear she's excellent. Maybe if Janelle puts in a good word, she'll work something out with you."

We called Janelle on Brianna's phone, and she three-wayed us to Vera, the coordinator. She was pretty much booked but assured Brianna that because she was a friend of Janelle's they could work something out. We scheduled a meeting with her for later in the week. The problem was on the way to being solved, but I was getting more involved in this wedding than I had planned. I would have to leave work early on Wednesday night for the meeting.

"Thank you, Nina," Brianna said. "I don't know what I would have done if you didn't help me out."

"Girl, it's no problem," I said. "Well, I guess that's all until Wednesday."

"Almost," she said. The look in her eyes told me that I was going to have to finally come clean with her. "Nina, I know that you don't really care for me, so I just want to sincerely thank you for being in my wedding and helping out like this."

"I like you, Brianna. From what I know about you so far, you seem cool."

"Maybe you think I'm cool, but be honest. You don't think I'm good enough for Brice."

"That's not it at all."

"Well, Nina, what is it? I love your brother with all my heart, and I'm looking forward to being with him for the long haul. I want to enjoy spending time with his family as much as he does with mine. And I do, but I just get the feeling that you don't want me with him."

I cleared my throat, preparing to say what I had been needing to get off my chest for some time. "You just don't understand what you're getting yourself into by marrying my brother. I mean, I love Brice too, but Brianna, I just don't want to see you becoming a miserable person because of who he is."

Although I was being honest, I felt guilty, like I was ratting out my brother. But she had given me the heads up earlier about Maurice, so I felt it only right to warn her about Brice. "You seem like a nice person, and to be honest with you, I think you'll be making a big mistake by marrying him."

"I don't think you understand—" she began.

"But see, I do understand," I interrupted. "I was born into my family. You don't know what I understand. You don't know anything about us."

"Listen, Nina, I'm trying to tell you that you've got it all wrong, what you think about Brice and me."

"You know what? You're going to believe what you want to anyway. I'm sure you can't see past that ring that's on your finger, so I'm not going to waste any more of my time or yours," I said, quickly pulling my money out of my purse.

Brianna looked disappointed, but so was I. How was I going to go down my family's history with her? Through my dreams and in-depth conversations with Janelle, I had begun to remember just how severely my dad used to beat on my mom. It had been difficult enough to accept that my dad was unfaithful; now I knew he was physically abusive as well. I didn't have the patience or the energy to talk about it, especially with someone who wouldn't think that what my mother had endured and still goes through could happen to her.

"Good-bye, Brianna," I said.

She sat there looking dumbfounded.

I placed the money on the table and walked out of the restaurant.

•   •   •   •

I felt badly about the way I walked out on Brianna, but I had to do it. She probably thought I was a bitch. And she had every right to. I was rude, and for no reason. I couldn't call her to apologize because she would want to talk, and frankly, I didn't want to discuss it, not with her. I wanted to call Leo but didn't want to bother him with my problems. And with the news of Maurice being in town, I wasn't ready to face Leo. So I called Janelle. Maybe she'd at least be able to shed light on my dilemmas.

I tried a few times to reach her before I gave up. She probably wouldn't have understood why I blew up at Brianna anyway, and she would have told me not to even think about going back to Maurice. So maybe it was a good thing she wasn't home. I had to deal with my issues myself. I didn't need any help, I thought. I'm a grown woman, with my own job, my own place, and my own bills. Surely I have the maturity to deal with my own problems.

My pep talk sunk in, and I pushed the worries of my day to the back of my mind and spent the rest of the evening planning my schedule and lining up contact information for the upcoming week. I decided to let the chips fall where they would, I'd have to see Brianna on Wednesday, and I would deal with her then. And as far as Maurice was concerned, if he wanted to contact me, he knew the number.

Eighteen

Janelle and I stood in line at will-call on a warm Friday night to get our all-access passes for Leo's concert. I was thrilled to see such a great turnout. Hot 97.5, the hip-hop radio station, had been promoting the concert for two weeks by playing Leo's single from his debut album. Leo spent an hour with the morning deejay, and the listeners responded positively to his music. One listener called because she was amazed to find out that he had released two albums overseas and it had taken him three years to premiere in the U.S. It was obvious from the early reviews of his album and the hometown support, which was hard to come by, that Leo was well on his way to becoming a hit in the States. I was probably more excited than he was.

"Now, this is the side of you I like to see," Janelle said as we walked toward the entrance.

"It's long overdue," I replied happily. I had spent the past couple of weeks worrying about Brianna. It got worse when Brice called and insisted that I stop by the spa so we could talk. I'd been watching the caller ID, dodging Brice's calls, while hoping and waiting to hear from Maurice.

The meeting with Brianna and Vera went smoothly and Brianna

didn't mention my behavior at brunch. Vera was extremely professional and from that point on really helped Brianna get a grip on her wedding plans. With her on board, Brianna hadn't asked for my help since I met with them, but then again, I hadn't offered either.

I knew that Brice wanted me to like her and show my acceptance. My heart ached when I thought about the relationship we could have had if I had put forth effort, but a part of me didn't want to try because I didn't want to be too close when all hell broke loose between her and Brice. I didn't want to reexperience the pain of not being able to help someone out of a bad situation with someone I loved. I wanted to remain hands-off, and maybe in some weird way I wanted to argue with her, so I didn't have to become chummy.

Leo's concert would be the respite that I needed to forget my shortcomings, and I intended to totally immerse myself in the evening. Being at the Atrium enjoying the fruit of Leo's labor assured me that if all else fell apart, I still had a strong man who cared for me. Since we had made love, things had begun to move along smoothly between us.

"Nina Lander!" Someone yelled my name from the line that was forming at the box office. I turned around to see who it was. I didn't recognize the face.

"Do I know you?" I asked.

"I'm just a fan," the guy said. "I watch you on the news. You're one of my favorite reporters."

"Thank you," I said, and a few other people in the line waved. I waved back.

I was flattered. I guess I'd been so involved with covering the local news and keeping my personal life intact that it hadn't occurred to me that my face had become recognizable.

"Hey, Miss Popularity. You want to show the man your pass?" Janelle joked.

We laughed. I showed my pass, and we walked into the club.

Leo had told me that it would be a good idea to hang out in VIP for a while and go backstage thirty minutes before his performance because he wouldn't be getting to the club until then. We wandered around the club and in and out of VIP. Janelle got a kick out of being able to move about freely without any hassle.

"This is the way partying should be," she said.

I agreed.

The place was packed solid, and the deejay was playing hit after hit record. We decided to get close to the dance floor and people-watch, when a set of twin brothers approached us and asked us to dance. We got on the floor, and the brothers were working it out. They had serious moves. They were dressed alike in nice-fitting slacks and vests, which they wore open to expose their chests. From their sexy moves and their hard bodies, I could guess their profession. I danced close to Janelle and said, "Girl, what are we doing dancing with a pair of strippers?"

She laughed. "Getting our grooves on!"

"So, how long have you two been stripping?" I asked my dance partner.

"About two years," he replied.

"Are you good at what you do?" I asked.

"The best," he said. He nudged his brother and winked, and they commenced to freaking us right there on the dance floor.

Normally I would have been embarrassed, but I was in such a good mood, and these guys were fun. I looked over at Janelle and slapped her a high five. They calmed down.

"So, how would you rate us?" my partner asked.

"Definitely a ten!" I replied enthusiastically.

We danced with them for a few songs. I took their card. The entertainment for Brianna's bachelorette party was sealed. We went back into VIP and had drinks until it was time to go backstage. I wanted to check my makeup before the concert, so we made our way through the crowd to the ladies' room and freshened up. On the way out of the rest room, Janelle was talking about how much she wished Tim had more free time when we ran into Maurice and Ian. Talk about a surprise. I knew I would see him eventually, but not at Leo's concert, of all places.

I was at a loss for words, and I think Janelle and Maurice were too. Luckily for all of us Ian didn't seem to be fazed by seeing us.

"Hey, ladies," he said, "need any help with your tire tonight?"

After an awkward moment, Janelle said with a laugh, "That's not funny. We don't want to be jinxed."

"How are you?" he said, and hugged Janelle.

"I'm fine!"

"I already know that."

"Oh, stop!" Janelle said, playing with her hair.

"And you?" he said, giving me a hug.

"Never better!" I replied.

"Hi, Nina, Janelle," Maurice said looking apprehensive and un-sure of what to do. He followed Ian's lead and hugged Janelle first, then me, but he didn't let me go.

"I'm sorry for the way things ended between us," he whispered in my ear.

How do you respond to words you've been waiting for so long to hear? I didn't say anything, because I wasn't sure if he was on a guilt trip, or if he meant he wanted to start over and try and work things out. I wanted to be sure before I put myself out there.

"Can I call you?" he asked.

I swallowed. Another surprise. He never failed to send me flying on an emotional roller coaster.

He released me from our embrace and waited for an answer. "You're a grown man, you can do whatever you want to do," I said, so as not to give permission.

"I'm going to take that as a yes," he said.

Janelle interjected. "So, are y'all visiting for the weekend?" I ap-preciated the rescue.

"Nah, I'm staying here for the summer," Maurice answered.

"Yeah, and I took a week's vacation to come and hang out with my man here," Ian said.

"When do you go back?" Janelle asked.

"Tomorrow morning," Ian replied.

"Have you enjoyed your stay?" I asked.

"I wish I could stay longer."

"So, what are you two doing here, tonight?" Maurice asked. "I didn't take you for the hip-hop types."

"We went to high school with LJ Love, and we came to see him," I replied. Janelle cut her eyes at me.

"Oh. Well, have a good time, and expect to hear from me soon, Nina," he said. They walked into the men's room.

I knew Janelle was going to ask why I downplayed my relationship with Leo. Before she could get the chance, I said, "Don't even ask."

When we got backstage Leo was there with his manager and some record-label executives. He appeared relaxed and self-assured. "There she is," he said as we approached him. He hugged and kissed me. "Nice choice," he said of my attire. "You are rocking the hell out of that dress."

"Thank you."

"Hey, Janelle, how are you?"

"I'm having a ball," she replied.

"Good. I'm glad you could make it out."

"Now you know I wouldn't be anyplace else tonight."

"Did your brother make it?" he asked me.

"No, he didn't. He had an engagement to attend with Brianna," I said. It wasn't a complete lie. My mom had informed me that he and Brianna had plans for the evening, but I didn't call to give him an option. "So, are you ready to go out there and do your thing?" I asked him.

"You know it," he said. "Let me introduce you two around."

There were a few producers there who I had met in the studio earlier in the year, but the others were new faces. The energy backstage was really positive, and it felt good just being around it. Everyone appeared calm and loose and ready for a good show.

Before long Leo was onstage. With his powerful stage presence, sheer talent, and performance savvy, he mesmerized the audience. Knowing that I was the one he loved made me feel lucky. So how come I couldn't stop thinking about Maurice? I couldn't justify to myself why, but I was still in love with him, and would never be able to completely commit to Leo until I got Maurice out of my system. Leo and I had a connection that I had never experienced with any other man, but it was Maurice's heart I was after.

Nineteen

Maurice called the next morning. I was still in bed, and Leo had spent the night. It was awkward picking up the phone and hearing his voice on the other end while my boyfriend was lying next to me naked.

"Hey, baby, it sure was good to see you last night," he said.

"Who is this?" I asked, stalling for time to compose my thoughts.

"Maurice, of course."

"Oh . . . how are you?"

"Been thinking about you ever since I saw you last night. Let's spend the day together. You know, talk and catch up."

"Well . . ."

"I'm not taking no for an answer," he insisted.

"I'm not sure if I can."

"Nina, I know you're probably pissed at me. You have every right to be, but give me the opportunity to see you and make up for some of my mistakes."

"Okay," I said. I didn't want to stay on the phone too much longer because it would make Leo suspicious.

"I'll be at your place around twelve."

I looked over at the clock. It was nine-thirty. "Make it twelve-thirty or one."

"Twelve-thirty it is," he said. "I'm looking forward to it."

I hung up and looked over at Leo, who was awake and staring at the ceiling. I couldn't read his expression, but I'm sure guilt was written all over my face.

"Good morning," I said.

"Morning."

"Hungry?" I asked.

"Nah, I'm cool," he replied. "I was going to suggest that we go out to my mom's friends' place today. They have horses, and I thought it would be nice to spend the day together since I'll be leaving to go on tour Sunday."

"Oh, right," I said. I had forgotten he was leaving so soon.

"But you have plans, right?" he said.

"Well, I'm supposed to meet"—I swallowed to get my lie together—"Gus. We have to go over some footage that was shot, um, last week. There was a problem, and we have to figure out if we need to reshoot, or trash it." I couldn't believe how easily the lies flowed from my mouth.

"That's cool, but you will be free tonight, right?" He seemed skeptical about my response but remained calm.

I faked a yawn to cover my uncertainty. "I'll be free."

"There's a party that I have to go to. I want you to go with me. We can go out to eat first."

"That's cool," I said.

"I'm going to head back to my place." I could tell he was disappointed.

He dressed while I remained in bed. "Don't work too hard," he said. There was light sarcasm there, but I didn't call him on it because it would have meant being up-front about the call.

"I'll walk you down," I said.

"No, stay in bed. I'll see you tonight." He disappeared down the stairs.

I was overcome with guilt. How could I have kept something from

Leo? He had always been so honest with me. I had been as forthright as I could, though I was still harboring secrets and acting as if I came from this picture-perfect household because I was scared that he would look at me differently and run away, just as Maurice had.

Lying there in bed, I persuaded myself that seeing Maurice would be a good thing. For one, if things were really over between us, then I would get closure. But if we were destined to be together, then I'd know that too. Once I found out, I would come clean with Leo.

·   ·   ·   ·

Maurice arrived two hours late and immediately began to apologize. "Sorry I'm late, but it took a little longer than I expected to get this for you," he said, and pulled out a tennis bracelet.

I wanted to tell him where he could shove his gift, but he had more surprises for me.

"That's not all," he said, and walked outside to get two dozen red roses. I was so overcome with guilt for thinking he had stood me up when he was out shopping for me all the while. I took the roses, lay them on the kitchen counter, and thanked him with a hug. Although our embrace began innocently, something came over me. I didn't want to let him go. I held on tight, my mind becoming jammed with questions, hopes, fears.

"If I'd have known the flowers would be such a hit, I'd have brought them out first," he said.

In spite of the fact that it felt good to have him back and being so generous, it was also emotionally draining. I thought about all the bumps we ran across in our short-lived relationship, and I couldn't help being angry.

"So, what do you want to do? I'm yours for the rest of the day." Those words felt temporary, and if I couldn't have more, I didn't want him at all.

"Why do you think you can just break things off without warning and expect me to want to come back to you and forget about everything just because you shower me with gifts?"

"Whoa, Nina. Calm down."

"How can I calm down? All I've done from the beginning of our relationship was try to love you and do everything I could to make you feel like a king. And you just treated me like shit! I didn't deserve that, Maurice."

I expected him to lash back at me, but he simply took a deep breath and walked over to me looking dejected. "I'm sorry," he whispered.

I looked into his eyes. He seemed sincere, but I was still upset.

"I'm sorry," he repeated, and put his arms around my waist. He softly kissed my forehead, and my anger transformed into fear.

"But how can I trust that this won't happen again?" I asked.

"Nina, I'm human. I can't guarantee things will be perfect between us, but I'm willing to try to work on being back together."

I breathed a sigh of relief. That was all I needed to hear: that he was there to make our relationship work.

"Now come here," he said, grinning.

I pouted a bit but finally gave in to him, completely, right then and there on my sofa. We rushed to remove our clothes. Skipping foreplay completely, we jumped into the act of sex as if to make up for lost time.

Out of breath, he stopped to get a condom, and in that brief moment I thought of Leo. How could I do this to him? I would have to come up with a way to explain to him that Maurice and I decided to work things out. He'd have to understand, and if he didn't, it wouldn't matter, because at that moment nothing was as important as knowing Maurice wanted me back.

• • • •

I awoke the next morning to breakfast in bed. Overlooking my promise to meet Leo, I had spent the night at Maurice's apartment. Now I was plagued with guilt and disappointment in myself. I knew I should have handled the situation better by at least calling to cancel. But I was caught up in Maurice's world and didn't want to leave.

Leo would be flying out that day. Not wanting to upset him at the beginning of his tour, I decided to wait until he got back to tell him what was going on. But I had to at least say good-bye.

After eating breakfast, I got up. "I need to go," I said.

"So soon?" Maurice protested. "Let's stay in bed all day. It's a Sunday, what do you have to do?"

"Well . . ."

"Just stay. We can go to a matinee later."

I was swayed. "Okay, but I need to make a call to my friend who's going out of town today."

"Go ahead and use the phone," he said, then got up and put the plates on the tray. "I'll start washing the dishes, so come and help when you get off."

That was easy.

I called Leo, who wasn't in, and left a message on his voice mail. "Leo, I'm sorry about last night . . . I was hoping I'd catch you before you left, but I guess I called too late . . . Call me tonight, and I'll explain everything." I hung up, then called my voice mail. There were three messages from Leo. The first said, "What's up, kid? Where are you? Call me. I want to see you tonight." His tone was upbeat.

On call number two he sounded disappointed. "Nina, where are you? We did have plans. A call would be nice . . . but I guess something must have come up."

Message three came that morning. "I'm a little worried," he said in a monotone. "I hope everything's all right. I'm hoping to hear a good excuse. Well, I'll call you once I get settled into the hotel in New York."

I lay back in the bed. There was no way I could fix the damage I had done to Leo and me.

"Nina, are you still on the phone?" Maurice yelled from the kitchen.

"I'm off."

"Oh, so you're not gonna help a brother out?"

"Coming," I said. I hopped out of bed and rushed to assist the man who controlled my heart, hoping and praying he'd be worth sacrificing the best male friend I'd ever had.

. . . .

I fed Leo a lame excuse about working late and not being able to get to a phone. He said it was no problem. But it was obvious by the flow of the rest of our conversation that it was.

"Nina, our relationship is important to me, but I also have to remain focused in order for this tour to be a success," he said.

"I know," I replied.

"So, I need you to work with me and do two things for me."

"Okay."

"Baby, let's try to always consider that our time together, especially while I'm touring, will be limited," he began.

"I know."

"Right. So, let's commit to honoring that time. It might not always be easy, but let's try."

The guilt was eating away at me. I couldn't respond, so he continued after a brief silence between us. "The other thing is that I can't control you—I don't want to—and you can't control me. So let's love each other every day like it's our last chance, but allow the other to walk away if the other chooses to do so."

"Do you think I'm trying to leave you?" I asked.

"I didn't say that, baby. You know me. I like to lay it all out on the table, then move forward."

"Understood," I said.

"All right, so I'll talk to you soon."

"Okay." I hung up and fell on my bed and cried. I didn't want to be putting Leo through my drama, but I couldn't bear to be honest about Maurice. I wasn't sure what would happen with him. He was so unpredictable. I hurt for Leo's feelings and I felt sorry for myself, because at that moment I realized that I was no better than my father. I hated the person I had become, but I couldn't stop myself. I wanted Maurice's affection whatever the cost.

While Leo was on the road I spent a lot of time at Maurice's house. I began to call less often. So did Leo. He must have grown tired of talking to my voice mail, and of me returning his calls in an untimely manner, often missing him entirely and throwing out excuse after excuse.

All the while I was going out of my way to keep Maurice's attention. I no longer took extra assignments at work, reporting only what was required of me. I hadn't spoken to Janelle since Leo's concert and continued to dodge Brice. I didn't even find time to stop by and visit my parents. I wanted to keep Maurice happy and was determined to do whatever was necessary.

Twenty

Maurice and I had been inseparable for almost two months, but over the past week it had taken longer for him to answer my pages. Lately when we talked, he was shorter with comments and general conversation. Although I denied it, he was beginning to go back to his inconsiderate ways.

I began coming up with ideas to capture time from him. That Friday I awoke early, prepared for my day, then called him before I left for work.

"I have something planned for us after I get off work," I announced.

"I don't know. I'm not sure what I'm supposed to be doing this evening."

"Spending it with me," I told him. I could feel the desperation creeping in my throat.

"I don't know. Call me when you get off work and we'll see," he said vaguely. I, however, heard something else.

"You be ready, because you don't want to miss my surprise," I said in my most persuasive voice.

"We'll see."

I wanted to rush through my workday, but it seemed like the more anxious I became, the slower the hands on the clock seemed to move. When I finally got home, I didn't take off my shoes or sit and relax for a moment but ran to page Maurice, then awaited his call.

I waited for over two hours. I knew it was that long because after I paged him, then left messages on his home voice mail and two cell phones, I planned my schedule for the week and researched a story I'd be doing on the benefits of the new baseball stadium. The story had already been covered, but the station figured I could find something new to say. After spending a couple of hours on the Internet looking for pertinent information, I stopped, irritated because I hadn't heard from Maurice. So I paged him again, and he finally called.

"Nina?"

"Maurice?"

"Who else would it be?" he asked. He sounded frustrated.

"Well, I wasn't sure. After all, it's been over two hours since I paged."

"Yeah, I know, but I was tied up. So what's up?"

I couldn't believe he asked that question. "I'm wondering the same thing," I replied.

"Well, you paged twice. You never page twice, so I assumed it was urgent."

"No, it's not urgent." I resisted the urge to raise my voice, because I didn't want to ruin my chances of seeing him or to start an argument. Softening my approach, I said, "So, when do you think you'll find time for your girlfriend who misses you so much?"

He replied, "Not sure. I've been spending long hours conditioning. I have to up my game for next season. Plus, some of my teammates are going to be in town tomorrow and I have to show them around. And I'm working with my agent to secure an endorsement deal." He paused and let out a long sigh. "Baby, I'm worn out."

"Oh!" That's all I could get out. I was being blown off, and the hurt took away my words. Granted, he had a trying schedule, but I know that it's human nature to make time for what's important to you.

And it was blatantly apparent that I was not a top priority on Maurice's list.

"And I'm not really sure if I'll get the opportunity to see you," he added.

I had to handle this situation delicately. I knew if I said the wrong thing, the conversation would end without me being sure where I stood with him. "Maurice, I understand you're tired and I know you're busy, but I really miss you." I paused to allow my words to sink in. "Why don't you call me when you're on your way home tonight, and I'll meet you there, give you a nice back rub and some unforgettable sex to help you sleep?"

"Did you not hear what I just said?" He spoke to me as if I were a child.

"Huh?" That about summed up the many feelings I was experiencing.

"I mean, why are you giving me such a hard time? You know I got a lot on me."

"Oh, so I'm giving you a hard time?" I dropped the nice-girlfriend role and called on my sistah-girl 'tude.

"Yeah, you are. I told you I'm extremely busy, but you insist on seeing me."

"So what are you gonna be so busy doing tonight?"

"Maurice doesn't have to answer to you!" he barked.

"Are you saying the relationship is over, because if that's what you're implying, just spit it out!" I yelled.

"See, there you go trippin'! I didn't say all that. I'm just saying I won't be able to see you at least until sometime next week."

"Oh, so I'm the one who's trippin'. I say I want to spend some quality time with my man, and I'm trippin'. I try to meet you halfway, compromise, say I'll come to your place tonight, no matter what time, but I'm trippin'. No, I'm not trippin'. You're trippin', 'cause you're hiding something and trying to make me look like the overbearing girlfriend in the process."

"See, there you go with those long speeches. I ain't got time to be listening to that noise."

"I'm not talking noise. I'm just stating the facts."

"Can we discuss this at some other time?"

"No, 'cause it's an issue now," I retaliated. It annoyed me the way he always ran from confrontation.

"There is no issue," he said impatiently.

"Yes, there is," I said. "After you finish with your responsibilities you have to go home and sleep, but for some reason you don't want me there with you. So I have to believe that either you want someone else there with you or you're going to be sleeping elsewhere. So which is it?"

"Nina, ain't nothing going on." Then he calmed himself. "I'll tell you what, if I'm not too tired when I get home tonight, which I doubt, I'll call you and you can come over."

"Oh, so now you're doing me a favor!"

"See, there you go again. I'm trying to compromise, but you want to continue arguing."

"What kind of compromise is that?"

"A logical one."

"Maurice, if you want out, just let me know."

"I just said that's not the case," he replied. "I got to go. Look, I'll call you . . . okay," he said, and hung up the phone.

I couldn't believe I'd just gotten played like that. Why didn't he just break up with me? Why would he want to stay with me if he didn't want to spend time with me anymore? Why not just be honest and tell me if he had somebody else?

But more important, why was I putting up with it? Leo loved me, and I knew he was the better man. Since the day I first had coffee with him, I knew he was the one I should have been focusing on, but I couldn't because my heart wouldn't cooperate with my mind.

.   .   .   .

When it comes to limiting their emotional involvement in relationships most men are smart because they're not big on playing the waiting game. So many of us women, on the other hand, have mastered the art of waiting for the men in our lives. We secretly wait all day in anticipation of a call that's not expected until evening. We wait for men to leave their wives. We wait for our men to get their playing-the-field days out of their systems, hoping for a commitment, a proposal, a wedding. We play the waiting game because we're impatient for love. I was no exception. I had been waiting all evening for my so-called man to call. I wouldn't leave the house and continuously eyed the phone like a mouse does cheese.

I didn't dare call Janelle for support because I could only imagine what her advice would be: "Forget about him and just move on." But it wasn't that easy.

Since we had talked several hours had passed and I'd called Maurice's house four times and paged him. The more he ignored me the more obsessed I became. I went over the relationship from the beginning, remembering the good and the bad. But especially the good. How he'd always told me how much he cared for me. Our intimate moments, like when we made out at the park in D.C. I could hear the airplanes landing smoothly across the river while we were softly exploring each other's pleasure zones. It was different from what Leo and I had. It was daring, exciting.

I wanted that feeling back. I didn't know where I stood with him, which is why I felt like I had nothing to lose by calling and paging and paging and calling. And that's what I planned to do all night until I spoke with him.

•　　•　　•　　•

I woke up and found myself in my living room, struggling to separate reality from the crazy dream I'd just had. Maurice was signing autographs, and there was a mob of people around him. I fought my way through the crowd to get to him. When I got to the middle of the crowd, he was gone. I looked over my shoulder and saw him being driven away in a long white limousine. I got into my car and followed, but I lost sight of his car and was on a long road I didn't know. It had no exits, no signs. I felt lost. I was lost.

I sat up on the sofa. The television was blasting, and a hot new video by Will Smith was on. He looked so at peace with his success. I, on the other hand, felt like I was just beginning to understand my life. Would I ever be at peace with myself?

I looked at the clock. It was 2:00 A.M. Maurice hadn't called. I began to feel the rage that had lulled me to sleep. So, of course, I called him.

He answered in his groggiest, I'm-asleep-so-why-are-you-calling-at-this-time-of-the-night voice. I was irate. How dare he be cozy and comfy, while I was awake, in the middle of the night, recovering from anxious dreams and wondering about him?

I managed to say, "Did you forget to call?"

"Nina?" he asked. "Are you crazy? Why have you been blowing up my pager, and why are you calling me at all hours of the night?"

"No, the question is why didn't you call me, or better yet, why didn't you answer the phone?"

"I turned it off because I'm trying to get some sleep. Listen, can we continue this tomorrow?"

"No, we can't."

"I don't want to hang up in your ear, so I'm just gonna say bye and put the receiver down," he said almost too calmly.

"Maurice, we need to talk!"

"Okay, but not now."

I heard a voice in the background asking who was on the other end.

"Yes, now," I demanded.

"Bye, Nina," he said, and hung up the phone.

I knew I wasn't being rational, but who had time to be rational when love was at stake? I had to do something. I was too angry to cry. I knew Maurice had a bitch in his apartment. And it was my duty to let her know that although he was sexing her up that night, he was in a relationship with me. However screwed-up, it was a relationship.

The wine on the rack was calling my name. I reached for a bottle and a corkscrew and popped it open, and began to devise a plan to warn the girl at Maurice's house of what she was getting herself into.

After about an hour I had finished off the bottle and had the courage to go through with my plan: SAVE THE GIRL FROM MAURICE!

Twenty-one

The cab let me off at the curb and drove away, and there I was, standing in front of Maurice's apartment, drunk.

It was a luxury apartment community in Buckhead. I walked up the outside stairs to the second floor of his place, then banged on the door and rang the bell like a heathen. I was sure Maurice saw me through the peephole and chose to leave me outside with my ignorant behavior.

After not getting a response and feeling defeated, I wandered the grounds until I found myself outside the clubhouse. It was as deserted as my heart felt, so I sat right in front of the entrance and began to sob uncontrollably. I sobbed for myself, for my mother, for Brianna—even for the unsuspecting girl in Maurice's apartment. I cried until I blacked out or fell asleep.

I awoke to a warm southern breeze. Unsure how much time had elapsed, I reached into my purse to see the clock on my cell phone. It was 5:30 A.M. What in the hell was I doing waking up outdoors at five-thirty in the morning!

The pain that had lulled me to sleep was now anger. I hated all men! And I was being victimized by their conniving leader, Maurice.

He had taken my heart and used it as a doormat. He'd bought it because it looked suitable to walk over.

I was frightened. I needed someone to have my back, because I no longer wanted to take responsibility for my actions. My fingers began dialing Janelle's number. She would stop me from going too far.

"Hello!" she answered.

"Janelle!"

"Hello, who is this?"

"Janelle, I need you to come and get me!" I was out of breath and could hear the hysteria in my voice.

"Nina, is that you?"

"Yes! Please . . . that bastard has lost his damned mind, again! I need to get out of here, now!"

"Where are you?"

"I'm in front of the clubhouse, around the corner from Maurice's apartment."

"What are you doing at the clubhouse at this hour?"

"Janelle, does it matter?" I snapped. "Just come now," I demanded, then gave her the address and directions.

"Okay, I'm on my way, but you've got a lot of explaining to do."

"Okay, but hurry."

I paced back and forth in front of the clubhouse, waiting. I walked around back, where one of the community's three pools was located. I wandered over to the pool house, and to my surprise the door was open. I went inside and grabbed a towel, washed my face, and rinsed my alcohol-tainted breath. I felt anxious, because although Janelle was on her way, I knew I wasn't leaving the grounds without a confrontation with Maurice. I stared at myself in the mirror, disgusted by my reflection. I had become an insane person who would go to any lengths to prove myself to a man who obviously didn't care how much I needed his love.

What was scarier was the realization that I couldn't stop myself. Sitting on a bench, I tried to figure out a way to get Maurice to come to the door. Once I came up with a plan, I got up and walked out of the pool house.

I took my time and walked back toward his apartment. Along the way I heard birds chirping, signaling the dawn of a new day. But I was still stuck in yesterday. As I got closer I could see Janelle parking her car. She got out, walked up to Maurice's door, and rang the bell. There was no answer. She walked back to the edge of the lawn as I came around the side of the building.

"Girl, what took you so long?" I asked.

"Where are you coming from?" Janelle asked, looking behind me to get a clue.

"I waited in the pool house."

"What's going on?" Janelle said. "You look terrible!" Although I had attempted to clean my face, it was still makeup-stained. My hair was untamed, my clothes were wrinkled.

Still in a daze, I didn't answer. My focus quickly went back to the door of Maurice's apartment.

"Come on, let's get in the car," Janelle said. "We can talk in there."

"I can't leave," I cried.

"What? Where is Maurice?"

"He's inside, but I can't leave. Not now. . . ." I dropped down and sat in the middle of the manicured grass. I didn't care if I stained the seat of my pants. If I had to, I was going to camp right there until that coward came out. He'd have to leave sometime. I stared past Janelle and went into a trance. Physically I was there, but mentally I was at a place I was beginning to know all too well. It was the lonely, frightened state I found myself in every time I had a fight with Maurice, a painful place of overwhelming emotions, leading, eventually, to numbness.

"What are you doing? We need to go." Janelle seemed confused and frustrated by the situation she had walked into.

"Janelle, go get him. He won't come out and talk to me," I said, and rested my head on my knees.

"I already knocked on the door. No one's home. Let's get into the car and I'll take you home." I must have weirded her out, because she began to handle me carefully.

"No, that's not home. This is supposed to be my home . . ."

"Well, why are you outside? Let's go to my place and you can come back here when Maurice gets back."

"He *is* in there. Please, make him let me in!" I jumped up off the ground and ran to the front door. I leaned my back and head against the door and stomped my right foot against it. The banging sound echoed through the air, disrupting the neighborhood's morning peace, but I couldn't stop. I kept banging and banging with my foot.

Janelle's mouth was wide open. She was at a loss for words and didn't know what to do. I'm sure she was thinking her friend was out of her mind.

Suddenly the door flew open and Maurice grabbed me by my arms, ran down the steps, and threw me on the lawn. He hovered over me and began squeezing my neck, choking me. Gasping for air, I could scarcely breathe. Janelle tried to pull Maurice off me, but he got up and lifted his fist at her. She jumped back.

"You step back, if you know what's good for you," he barked.

"I don't know what's going on, but this doesn't involve me, Maurice," she yelled. Then she pulled out her cell phone and began to dial. "I'm calling the police," she said.

I had found my moment to get to whoever was inside his apartment. I jumped off the ground and began running toward the front door.

Maurice must have heard movement behind him because he abruptly turned to see what was going on. Although I was running with all my might, he managed to catch me. Again I was on the ground with Maurice's hands around my throat. This time I managed to knee him in the groin, and he fell on his back. I jumped on top of him and began scratching his arms and his face. He tried to push me off him, so I bit his arm. He yelled and threw me off him. We both lay in the middle of the ground, huffing and panting like wild animals.

I sat up and looked at Maurice's apartment. "I need to talk to her."

"Go home, Nina!" he yelled.

"I just need to talk to her."

I could tell Janelle was scared. She didn't know what she was supposed to do at that point, so she just watched the dog-and-cat fight, from a distance.

Maurice sat up. "Just go home," he said to me in a quiet, controlled voice. "Janelle, please come and get your friend and take her home!"

Maurice's sudden calmness snapped Janelle out of her trance, and she slowly walked over to the wheezing, crying, deranged stranger I had become. She crouched down beside me and grabbed my arm. "Let's leave," she said firmly.

I looked over at Maurice. "Please, I just want to talk to you."

"No," he said sternly. "You need to go home."

"But I love you! I need to talk to you."

Maurice looked at me with disgust in his eyes. I knew he disapproved of my actions, but I also knew that despite everything he cared for me, and he knew he had helped drive me to behave this way.

"Maurice, please," Janelle interjected. "I don't know what's going on here, but please, just talk to her."

Maurice huffed.

"Maurice, look at her," Janelle said, looking deeply concerned.

"Okay, you have five minutes," he said to me.

"Can we walk?" I asked. I even disgusted myself. I should have known that was my time to walk away. But I couldn't find the strength to do so.

He sighed. "O-okay." We got up off the ground, and I grabbed his hand tightly as we walked toward the back of the building.

"Maurice, please tell me you love me," I begged. "I need to hear those words."

He became a wall, stone silent.

"Talk to me!" I pleaded.

"You're the one who wanted to talk. I have nothing to say. You have five minutes, so you talk."

"Who's that chick in the house? And why is she there?"

"Look, Nina, I told you not to come over. I told you I would call you later, but you came over anyway. You didn't respect my request, so I don't have to explain anything to you."

"Who is she?"

"Like I said—"

"So are you saying it's over between us?" I asked.

He was a wall again.

"Do you love me?" I asked.

"I think your five minutes are up," he said, then grabbed my hand and walked me to Janelle's car. I was so desperate to show him how much I needed him, so I turned away from the car and threw my arms around his waist. He put his hands on his hips and stared at the sky, emotionlessly.

He walked with me wrapped around him and opened the car door, peeled me off him and attempted to put me into the passenger side. "Bye, Nina."

Janelle began walking toward the driver's side when the stranger who had taken over my body fell to her knees, wrapped her arms around Maurice's legs, and screamed, "Please tell me you love me . . . please!"

Janelle walked over and picked up my shell. I fell limp into her arms. She and Maurice put me in the car in silence, and we drove off.

I was defeated. I had humiliated myself, my womanhood. I walked away insecure, helpless, alone, scared, and slightly deranged. But instead of seeing what I had done wrong, I became a victim, asking why he no longer wanted me. What was wrong with me? Wasn't I lovable? Wasn't I worth a decent explanation for what happened? Wasn't I worth the closure that I so badly needed but for the life of me couldn't get?

I leaned back in the seat, closed my eyes, and sat in motionless silence until we reached my apartment. I hoped that when I chose to open my eyes again I'd realize that it had all been a horrible dream.

Awakening

Twenty-two

"Why haven't you returned any of my calls?" Brice demanded as he walked through my door. "The wedding is in less than a month, and you haven't had the decency to get back to me." He wasn't his usual cheerful self. There were no jokes, just my brother appearing more serious than I'd ever remembered seeing him.

"I'm sorry," I said, and sat down on the sofa. I was still in my bathrobe. My head was throbbing from a hangover, and my heart was aching from the night's fiasco.

"You could have at least phoned Brianna to see if she needed anything, and Nina, if you didn't want to be her maid of honor, you could have said so to spare yourself and us the unnecessary drama."

"Yeah, right," I replied under my breath.

"And furthermore, why haven't you stopped by to see how Mom is doing?"

"Why should I? I already know how she's doing—miserable. Every time I go over there I leave feeling worse than if I didn't."

"That's no excuse. She's your mother."

"And I love her dearly, but it's difficult to be around her sometimes."

"I can't believe those words are coming from your mouth. What did she ever do to you to make you feel this way?"

"She didn't do anything to me. It's what she's doing to herself, Brice. She's not living her life, and it eats me up to see her relinquish her power to Daddy. I've had to watch that recurring episode since I was a child." I sat up and attempted to make my point clearer. "On a daily basis I struggle with who I am. I question my self-worth. And last night I was in a physical fight with a man who doesn't even love me."

"Leo hit you?"

"No. I fought with Maurice."

"You did *what*? When I see that punk . . ." Brice jumped out of his chair and started pacing the floor. There was rage in his eyes.

"Calm down. He wasn't right, but I provoked him."

"There is no excuse to hit a lady, ever," he said with conviction.

"So, you're trying to tell me you never got physical with Brianna?" I asked.

"Not that it's your business, but no."

"Whatever," I said brushing his lie off.

"Now, if you ask if I've ever hit a woman, the answer is yes, but Brianna, I never have and I never will."

Before I knew it Brice was launched on a story I'd never taken the time to hear before—of how he and Brianna got together. He'd met her one night after he blew up at one of his old girlfriends, Donisha. He slapped her because she raised her voice at him.

"Even after I hit her she kept jumping in my face and arguing. My first instinct was to slam her on the ground, but instead I grabbed her by her neck and pushed her against the wall."

I was shocked at his confessing to me.

"I called her every degrading name I could think of. And the sad part about it is I wanted her to hurt and didn't stop until she was in tears."

I didn't know what to say.

"Afterward I felt guilty and hated myself for being so cruel, so I walked out. It wasn't the first time I did something like that, but that night affected me more than any other time before.

"I went to a bar-and-grill to have a drink to numb the pain. That's the night I met Brianna. She walked in to get change from the bartender to make a phone call. I was drawn to her, and we ended up talking all night."

"Really?"

"We talked about me and Donisha. Because of Brianna, the next morning I calmly called her to apologize for my behavior and told Donisha we weren't good for each other."

"Good for you. I wish all men could think like that." I said this with some bitterness, thinking of Maurice.

"Easy," he said, calming me down. "Although Donisha resisted the breakup, I walked away and never went back."

Brice told me that over time he became good friends with Brianna and shared his feelings about our father's abuse of our mother. He confided to her that he sometimes mistreated the women he dated. She told him that if he ever expected to have a relationship with her, he would have to see a therapist.

"I flat-out refused, so she stopped taking my calls. She told me that she couldn't be my therapist. That stumped me, Nina. No woman had ever been that bold in dealing with me."

I was riveted by his story and wished I could have been as strong as Brianna when it came to dealing with Maurice and his issues, or my own for that matter.

"At first I was mad at her, pissed," he said. "I tried forgetting about her, but I couldn't because I realized there was something different about her and that I cared for her."

"That's so sweet," I remarked.

"I knew the only way I'd be able to get close to her was to start seeing a therapist. So I called and asked her if she could suggest one. She helped me find an African-American male psychologist."

"Really? Brice, you've seen a psychologist?" I asked in disbelief.

"Yeah, I couldn't believe it myself. I tried to play it cool at first and act like I didn't have a problem, but it became obvious that he was qualified for the job, and with time I began to open up. In the process I realized a lot of things about myself and how Mom and Dad's relationship affected me in more ways than I thought. So when Brianna told you you didn't understand about us, she was on point. You didn't know. She wouldn't even go out on a date with me until I finished the program he placed me on. Talk about motivation."

I felt like a jerk. And judging from the night before, not only did Maurice need help, but so did I. I was in a bad state, being culprit to Leo and victim of Maurice. There were issues I needed to deal with, but I'd always had a way of justifying them. Now I knew I was a wreck. But how could I change? I couldn't even admit to my brother what I was going through. I was pleased to know that Brice and Brianna were probably going to be all right after all, but their stability didn't help my situation much. Things were dark for me, and there wasn't a flicker of light in sight. The only thing I could see in my near future was crawling back into bed and mourning for me and Maurice.

"Nina, be straight with me. What's been going on with you?" he asked. "Are you going to be in the wedding or what?" I felt like a kid answering to a parent.

"I already said I would," I answered defensively.

"Are you going to see Mom tomorrow?" Brice asked.

"Is she cooking?" I asked.

"I doubt it. She hasn't been feeling too well lately."

"Why didn't she call?"

"She did, but you haven't been answering the phone."

"What's wrong with her?" I asked.

"I think you need to go over and see her, so she can tell you what's going on with her." I had never thought of the possibility of my mother becoming ill.

"Why can't you tell me?"

"Well, she told me she wanted to talk to you," he said, shifting uneasily. "Nina, on this one I have to honor her request."

Twenty-three

$\mathcal{I}$ knew I needed to put my personal problems aside and go visit my mother. After Brice left I dragged myself upstairs, got dressed, and headed to my parents' house.

When I pulled into the drive, both cars were in the garage, which meant they were both home. I had hoped my dad wouldn't be there because my mom was more secretive in his presence. I took a deep breath to prepare for whatever I was going to hear.

My dad was sitting outside on the deck when I walked in. The house was eerily quiet.

"Hey, Daddy," I yelled through the glass door.

"Ninu, come on back."

I walked out onto the deck and sat down beside him. "Where's Mom?" I asked.

"She's upstairs," he answered. Then he stretched and yawned. He looked exhausted. "Why has it taken you so long to come over and visit?" he asked calmly.

No matter how I answered that question, I would have been reprimanded. So I changed the subject.

"Is she sleeping?" I asked.

"I'm not sure. I was just up there about an hour ago, and she was sleeping then."

"Daddy, what's wrong with Momma?" I asked.

"You mean to tell me your mother's been sick all this time and you don't know what's wrong with her?" He shot me the most disgusted look he'd ever given me.

"Well, it's not like anybody tells me anything around here," I said defensively.

"If you came over to see your mother more often, you'd know," he said, then stood up and stretched. "Go on up there and see how she's doing. I need a break anyway. I'm going to the store to pick up some things. You stay with her until I get back, you hear me?"

"Of course," I replied. He walked through the house, picked up his keys, and headed out the front door. A wave of fear overcame me. I was afraid to walk up the stairs to my mother's bedroom. I didn't want to face her, but I knew I had to. It couldn't be that bad, I thought. She probably just needed a break with the way she carried on around the house and waited on my dad hand and foot. "She's going to be just fine," I said aloud, mustering the courage I needed to make it up the steps.

I tapped on the door and pushed it open. I hadn't been in my parents' room in a while. Even when I stayed there with them before I found my own place, I had found no reason to go inside. The room was furnished with antiques. An old chifforobe in the corner held special memories for me. I got a warm feeling when I remembered playing dress-up, sneaking to put on the nice dresses my mother stored inside.

My mother was lying on the bed with her eyes open. "I was wondering when you planned on visiting your mother," she said. Her voice was weak, but she seemed pleased to see me.

I took a seat next to her on the bed and kissed her on the cheek. "There isn't much time, and there's a lot that I want to say to you," she said. "Maybe I should have told you when you first came home from school, but I didn't want to worry you, with you trying to get a new place and job and find a path for yourself."

She strained to sit up. "Help me with the pillows," she said. I quickly put several pillows behind her head to help her comfortably sit up. When I'd last spent time with my mother, on Mother's Day a few months ago, she was moving around freely. Now she almost didn't look like the same person. It was as if she had aged ten years.

"Mom, what's wrong with you?" I asked.

"Well, Nina, I have cancer."

"What?" I yelled, jumping to my feet. I stepped back to get a full look at her face—I wanted to make sure she was telling me the truth.

"I was first diagnosed a year after you went away. My doctor found a lump in my left breast."

"No," I said in disbelief.

"I had to have a lumpectomy, which was the removal of the growth and surrounding tissues in my breast. Then I went through chemotherapy shortly afterward. It worked, and the cancer actually went into remission, so I felt there was no reason to tell you."

My legs were becoming weak and I felt faint, so I sat down in a chair near the bed.

She continued. "I felt fine and back to my normal self. A few weeks before your graduation I felt a growth in my right breast. The cancer had spread to my spine."

I couldn't believe it. I didn't want to believe it. "So, you'll go through chemotherapy again, right? And then they'll remove the cancer and you'll be just fine."

"At this stage, it's not that simple. There's no way to contain the growth. The best the doctors can do now is try to help me remain comfortable while I ride it out to the end."

"To the end," I said frantically. "Are you saying you're gonna die?"

"We all are, Nina. So yes, I am. The doctors have given me less than a year." Mom was so calm, and that worried me. She had accepted the verdict and didn't even seem to be willing to fight it.

"So Brice and Daddy know?"

"Yes."

I became angry. "Why didn't anyone tell me? I think I had a right to know. Maybe I could have done something? I don't know, maybe—"

"I can't take back not telling you, but I'm still here, and there's so much I want to share with you before I go."

"How can you talk about this like you're moving to another state?" I yelled. I hopped out of my seat and began pacing. "Momma, you're talking about leaving me for good. You can't do that, not yet. There's still so much more that I want you to see me accomplish." I knew I sounded selfish, but it was because Dad would never appreciate me the way Mom did. I needed her. I also wanted her to live because I hoped I would one day see her stand up to her husband or do something special, just for herself.

"Come here," she said.

"No." I began to cry. My mind filled with memories of my mom through the years. I searched and searched and couldn't pull out any time when Juanita Lander had been happy. She'd never even seemed satisfied with her marriage. It was as if she tolerated the life that was laid out for her and never took the initiative to improve or alter it. Now she was going to die. How could I accept such a fate for her?

"Come closer, Nina."

I needed to keep my distance because I needed time to think. Going to her would mean that I accepted what she was saying to me.

"Nina," she said sternly. I stared at her. The look in her eyes calmed me, so I reluctantly surrendered and walked over to her. "Come closer," she insisted. I sat down beside her. She reached out and put her arms around me as I lay on her chest and wept. This is all a bad dream, I thought. All a bad dream.

Twenty-four

Change is inevitable. People work so hard to establish their careers, their social lives, and their relationships, only to meet the expected unexpecteds: separation, divorce, death. I had hoped that my parents' relationship would end with my mother temporarily separating from my father to wake him from his cruel way of being. Or that my dad would divorce my mother and go on with his life, allowing her to begin anew. I never would have thought the change that would inevitably occur between Smitty and Juanita be death.

I now understood Brice's rush to get married. I'm sure he and Brianna would have tied the knot sooner or later. While they diligently planned and prepared, I began to focus on slowing down my life. Leo had stopped calling altogether, and I felt I didn't deserve him anyway. So I didn't try to contact him. I wasn't sure of what I'd say if we talked, so I didn't waste his time.

I vowed to never see Maurice again, even if he approached me with a permanent plan to stay together. It wasn't that I'd suddenly stopped loving him, because I hadn't. Even after our terrible fight, I still cared. But I was emotionally drained and needed to focus my attention on making sure my mother's last days, in what I was beginning to view as a selfish and unfair world, were as comfortable as possible.

After a full workday I'd usually stay at my parents', so eventually I decided to give up my apartment. It was a difficult adjustment, but I had a lot of support. Brice and Brianna were at the house for extended periods on Sundays and Mondays. Janelle would swing by a few times a week. My schedule consisted of working all day reporting news, and helping my dad with Mom at night. He had been surprisingly helpful, until I moved in—at which time he shifted his attention to whatever life he had established outside the house.

Mom and I were becoming friends, and I treasured our time together. For the first time she actually shared stories of her life with me.

"When I first met your dad, he swept me off my feet," she said.

"Really?"

"Yeah. If you think he's handsome now, you should have seen Smitty twenty years ago. He was built like your brother, with that same smile."

"Did you chase after Daddy?"

"No. Maybe that's why he was so interested in me. So many of the other girls did. I think he saw me as a challenge. I was going to the city college, and he and a couple of his friends used to ride over and hang around on the campus. When I first met him, I thought he was a student. I was a quiet country girl, and Smitty had moved from St. Louis to stay with his grandmother. He was in the fast lane, and although I was intrigued, I was scared of him. But he was persistent, and that man charmed me all the way to the altar."

"So did you love him?" I asked.

"I loved your father then and I still do. I think back to some of the old times, and I smile."

Some evenings when she was feeling strong we'd go through photo albums and she'd give me the background of each picture. My mother was beautiful back then, hopeful and carefree, her future ahead of her. She said her biggest dream was to marry my dad, have a nice home in the suburbs and raise a family.

"My dreams came true," she said.

Could she really believe that about her life with my dad? But she had a right to see life however she wanted.

Eventually I confided to her the real story of Maurice and me. I crawled into bed next to her, just like I was a kid, and began to talk. She listened in silence, and when I was finished, I noticed tears falling from her eyes.

"Why are you crying?" I asked.

"I'm okay. Just get me a tissue."

I got out of bed and went to the bathroom to get her a tissue. As I took in the many bottles of medicine on the vanity, reality hit me again. My mom was sick and fighting for a few remaining days. I shouldn't have told her about Maurice, I thought. My mission was to help her experience comfort and joy, not pain—my dad had caused enough of that for her lifetime.

I returned with the tissue and sat down in the recliner, my place of refuge when things got too heavy. It was a comfortable enough distance from the bed and allowed me to catch my breath. Then Mom did something that surprised me. She told me the story of the first time my dad hit her. "I know you must often wonder why I've stayed with your daddy for all these years. Well, I have my reasons. He wasn't always abusive. He used to be kind and caring."

Although I wanted to hear the story, I knew where she was going and I wanted to stop her. I didn't want her to relive the pain. "Momma, you don't have to—"

"No, Nina, I want you to know. I need you to know."

I sat back and listened.

"Brice was nine months old," she began. "He wasn't even walking yet, and I was home taking care of him. We had just moved out of our one-bedroom apartment into a two-bedroom house we were renting in the Westside of downtown Atlanta. I was so glad to have the space. I had just changed his diaper and laid him down for his afternoon nap when your dad came in from work early.

" 'Why are you home so early?' I asked him.

" 'Can't a man come to his own house when he wants without having to go through the third degree?' he replied.

"I could see the stress written on his face. 'Smitty, is everything okay?' I asked.

" 'I'll be all right if you quit asking a million questions and go get me something to drink.'

"I was used to your dad being abrasive sometimes, but I was so worried about his being home early, that when I went to pour him a glass of lemonade, I grabbed a plastic cup instead of a glass. Well, when I went to hand the cup to him he just stared at me and didn't reach to take it, so I grabbed a coaster and sat it down in front of him. Nina, things moved so fast from that point forward, because I don't remember how he managed to be on the same side of the coffee table as me. Before I could take the next breath, your father had grabbed the cup of lemonade and poured it over my head.

" 'Don't you ever, ever serve me in a cup!' he yelled, eyes blazing.

"I was so scared that I ran toward the bathroom, but he followed me.

" 'I wasn't finished talking to you,' he yelled.

"When I didn't respond, he pushed me into the bathroom and I hit the door with my elbow. I can still feel the pain. Then he closed me in there with him, and I remember seeing his balled fist coming toward me. I guess I blacked out, because eventually I woke up in the bed next to Brice, who was screaming at the top of his lungs. I calmed him down and then got up and walked over to the mirror. My hair and body were sticky from the lemonade, and my face was bruised and swollen. I was so angry when I saw my condition, I felt like I hated him. So I rushed out of the room to go give him a piece of my mind. I found him sitting on the steps in back of the house.

" 'Look at what you did to me!' I screamed. But when I got closer, I saw he was crying.

"I opened the screen door and walked over to him.

" 'I'm sorry,' he said, sobbing. 'I'm so, so sorry.'

"Later I found out that he'd been laid off, along with several other employees at the factory where he'd worked for three years. He was worried about keeping food in the house and paying the bills. With all of that, the least I could have done was give him a glass instead of a plastic cup. From that day forward, I kept my mistakes with your father to a minimum. I wish I could say that was the only time he took his anger out on me, but it wasn't. I learned to be more responsible for my behavior."

I didn't say anything.

"Nina, you shouldn't have gone over to Maurice's house, causing all that commotion. A man is gonna be a man, and you have to give him that freedom. You were wrong."

I was baffled; I thought my mother and I had been making progress, that I was getting through to her and we were somehow connecting. I thought she'd have some words of encouragement for me, telling me I had been right for not calling, or that I did good by moving on. But there was no support from her. At least not the emotional help I so desperately needed. We were further apart than ever. She was so out of touch with reality, stuck in some kind of a time warp. I couldn't hear another word from her. I couldn't accept her justifying Smitty's behavior and putting herself down.

I cared about her too much to upset her and tell her I thought she was wrong, so I took a deep breath and stood up. "Mom," I said, "I want to continue this conversation, but I forgot to make an important call, and I need to do it before it gets too late." I left the room more depressed and desperate than ever. There were so many things about life that I didn't have a grasp on. The person I saw as my only hope for getting some kind of understanding of the cycle of abuse was going to leave me before either of us could help ourselves.

Even more disturbing, I longed to call Maurice, to tell him what was going on with my mother so that he would come back to help me ease the pain.

That night I dreamt that I was in a graveyard. I walked over to my dad, who was digging a grave with a shovel. Above the grave was a tombstone that had my mother's name on it. I begged him to stop digging, but he wouldn't. I ran to the stone and tried to remove it but somehow lost my balance and fell on my back into the open grave.

"Help me!" I yelled.

I could see people, including Maurice, Mom, Brice and Dad, but no one stopped to help me.

I awoke hysterical, my heart racing with fear. It was around

3:00 A.M. I jumped up to check on Mom. She seemed to be sleeping peacefully, but Dad wasn't in there with her.

I went downstairs, but he was nowhere to be found. Why was he not there?

Although I needed to be up early the next morning, I refused to go back to sleep. I didn't want to dream ever again.

Twenty-five

Vera, the wedding coordinator, pulled off the impossible. The wedding was beautiful and tasteful. That night at the reception Mom was so happy, the happiest I'd seen her since the announcement of the wedding. She wore a lavender dress and hat and appeared healthy. It was as if she had stored all her energy for that day. Her typical reaction to crowds was to blend in and not be noticed, but now she lingered as close as possible to the center of the action. Although it was Brice's and Brianna's moment, it was Mom's night too. Seeing her firstborn marry and become the head of his own household rewarded her efforts in raising him and affirmed her as a good mother. I stayed close by her side, sharing in her joy.

Dad, on the other hand, seemed a bit standoffish, preoccupied.

Janelle sat at the table with Mom, Dad, and me. We joked all night. Although Mom couldn't dance because of the damage the cancer had done to her spine, we sang along with the live band and danced in our seats. More surprisingly, Mom shared stories of Brice's mischief as a young boy to whomever seemed interested.

When Brianna threw the bouquet, Mom insisted that Janelle and I join the hopeful bachelorettes. I feigned enthusiasm, but I wasn't the least bit interested in the competition. Janelle, on the other hand, made it clear that the bouquet was all hers. Her determination paid off, and after nudging aside the young lady standing beside her, she reaped her reward. We walked back to the table laughing. It wasn't that Janelle really cared about getting the bouquet, she just loved the thrill of winning.

"Oh, Nina, I was hoping you'd catch the bouquet," Mom said.

"I don't think there was any hope for me or anybody else with Janelle being here. She was determined to catch the bouquet at all costs."

"Yep, and that's why I got it. Isn't it beautiful, Mrs. Lander?"

"It sure is," Mom said. "Now Janelle, do me a favor and make sure Nina gets the bouquet at your wedding. Can you do that for me?"

"You have my word. I'll aim it right at her."

As the night wore on, God's grace was slowing draining from my mother and she grew weary. Although she didn't want to leave, we both knew it would be better to exit early with dignity instead of later in agony.

We were sitting at the table, and I reached over to my dad and let him know Mom was ready to go. There was no hesitation. He hopped up and immediately went to his wife's aid, while I pulled Brice and Brianna away from the dance floor to say our good-byes.

"Brianna, we're going to go ahead and get Mom in," I said to her.

She smiled. "Sure." She and Brice followed me to our table. Things between Brianna and me had improved after my talk with Brice. I had a new respect for her, and she was pleased that I lightened up on my judgment of both her and my brother. Also, as a truce, I had thrown her a bachelorette party to remember. I think it worked.

"Hey, Mom, it's time to call it a night, huh?" Brice said, and leaned over to kiss her on the cheek.

"Good night, Mom," Brianna said to her.

"I had a wonderful time," she said. "Now you two enjoy your honeymoon and take plenty of pictures and bring them back for me to see."

"We will," they assured her.

"Son, you need anything?" Dad said, reaching for his wallet.

"Everything's straight," Brice replied.

Brice looked back at Mom. I watched him closely, and I could see the pain in his eyes through the smile he gave her. "I'll bring those pictures back to you first thing!" he said.

"Okay," she said. "I love you two."

My heart grew heavy. I hoped she'd hold out to see those pictures.

Twenty-six

*I*t's amazing how it sometimes takes a word from someone on the outside of a situation to wake an individual from sleepwalking and make them see things from another perspective. On the day Brice and Brianna were to return from their honeymoon in Hawaii, Janelle stopped by the house to have brunch on the deck with Mom and me. I had invited her because although Mom seemed content inside, I thought it would be nice for both of us to spend some time outside our world, and Janelle always brought a new kind of energy into the house.

It was a humid yet beautiful Atlanta summer day, and I put the umbrella on the deck table and set up a jam box outside with some of my mom's favorite CDs. By the time Janelle arrived, I had muffins in a basket, a fruit bowl prepared, and omelets ready to be served. She helped me bring Mom down and get her comfortable on the deck. It took some effort, but it was well worth it to see the way Mom responded to the fresh air and sunshine. The yard wasn't as well kept as usual; since Mom had fallen ill, Dad hadn't stayed on top of it.

The doctor had told me that Mom could suddenly take a turn for the worse and need to be hospitalized. I dreaded that reality and was thankful to God every day that all seemed well.

Janelle stayed outside with Mom while I brought out the food and some freshly squeezed lemonade. By the time I sat down, Janelle and Mom had already launched the first topic of discussion.

"Mrs. Lander, I don't care what you say. Wesley Snipes is finer than that Denzel Washington."

"No, child, Denzel is the epitome of a good-looking man," Mom said. "What do you think, Nina?"

"Well, Mom, I have to agree with you. Denzel is handsome, there's no denying that, but Wesley is single, which makes his stock just a bit higher." I filled her plate and my own. Janelle followed suit.

"You girls must be blind, because there's no competition for those of us who have good vision."

"Now I do have to say, Denzel seems to be good to his wife, and I gotta give a brother credit for that," Janelle interjected.

"You don't know what's really going on behind closed doors," I said.

"See, that's your problem, Nina. You think men don't have the capability of being good to women."

"You're right. With the exception maybe of Brice, who is a reformed dog, men are no good. And I honestly wouldn't be surprised if he relapses and goes back to his old ways once he gets comfortable with the idea of being married to the same woman."

"What about Leo?" She went there.

"What about him? As far as I know Leo is still on tour, traveling somewhere, and I haven't received a call from him in months."

"He's a good man. Only you never gave him the opportunity to prove it to you."

"Leo is an entertainer. Good man and entertainer don't go in the same sentence," I retaliated. Deep down I knew I was wrong to say that about him, but I didn't want to accept that I'd lost a legitimately good man.

"Mrs. Lander, why is your child's mind so warped?" Janelle asked my mom, who seemed content to stay out of our argument.

"You might not want to hear what I have to say on the subject," my mom said, and took a sip of her lemonade.

"Yes, I would. It's always good to hear another person's perspective."

"I see things similar to Nina. My father was abusive to my mother, and so was her father to her mother. So, when all you know are men who degrade, put down, and mistreat the women you know and love, you have no other choice but to see it that way. Maybe there are some good men walking around somewhere on this earth, but even if they have intentions of doing right, they always eventually take a turn for the worse."

Janelle looked stunned. I don't think she was prepared for a dose of my mother's reality, the reality I had grown up in and adopted as my own.

"Mrs. Lander, I'm sorry you see it that way. It's unfortunate, because there are good men, those who make it their mission to be good and faithful husbands and fathers."

"But where are they?" I asked.

"It's my opinion that if you think the worst of people, you'll always find the worst people. But on the other hand, if you know there is good, you'll eventually run into the good ones." Janelle took her time to organize her thoughts. "I can name several men who are, quote unquote, good men. For example, there's my Uncle Clinton. He's been married to my Aunt Mildred for nearly fifty years, and he still holds her hand, reads to her at night, and sends her flowers just because. They've always been a positive example of a good couple for me."

"Okay, that's one, probably a fluke," I said defensively.

"The list goes on, but I'll have to use my own parents. When you live with people, you know what's really going on. And their relationship is on the up-and-up. They work as a team."

"I'm glad for your parents," my mother said. "But that just hasn't been my experience. Seeing is believing, and I was never given the opportunity to experience such a luxury." She looked off into a faraway place. I could only imagine where her thoughts were.

"It's not too late," Janelle insisted.

"Girl, stop talking nonsense," my mother said.

"I'm not. I don't know the whole deal between your husband and you, Mrs. Lander, but I can tell you this. You may not be able to change what has transpired between the two of you during the course of your marriage, but you can change what you will accept from him."

I was amazed to hear Janelle talk to my mother as if she were talking to me—woman-to-woman, without regard to their age difference. I could never have spoken to my mother like that. And Juanita seemed to be paying attention.

She continued, "You can let him know that you're aware he should have treated you better through the years. And that he's making a serious mistake if he doesn't recognize it for himself."

Mom clung to Janelle's words. "Do you think it would be worth it, especially after all these years?"

"Well, Mrs. Lander, only if you think you're worth it," Janelle responded.

"Ump," was my mom's response.

I was sure Janelle's words had hit home in more ways than one. My mother was more open than I'd given her credit for being. I had always assumed that because she was so private she'd be closed to an outside opinion. Giving it more thought, I realized my mother had never allowed herself the access to an outside opinion. She rarely watched television and had no real friends. She wasn't particularly close to her older brother, who lived in Arizona. We only saw him every two years or so. I'm sure Janelle's advice was the best she'd heard; more than likely it was the only womanly advice she'd received in quite some time.

I was thankful that although I hadn't realized I could have shared my opinion with my mother, Janelle couldn't see it any other way. I loved her for that and on that day thanked God for bringing such a good friend not only into my life but into my mother's.

•   •   •   •

That evening Brice and Brianna stopped by with pictures from their honeymoon.

"We stopped off at the one-hour photo place as soon as we got back into town," Brice proudly announced. "Once we got settled in, we picked them up on our way to you."

"Come on, sit beside me and give me details," she said to her son and daughter-in-law, patting the bed.

They sat on the side of the bed that I had thought of as mine, but I didn't mind. I felt full, because I was sure that my mom was also filled with joy. I took a seat in the recliner and watched the scene from a distance, overcome with love for the three of them. At the same time I felt resentment toward my dad, who was out as usual and missing such a special moment. I made up my mind that if Mom wasn't going to say anything to him, I would.

Twenty-seven

The change in my mother's condition that the doctors warned me of finally came. It was late one evening, and thank goodness, Dad was home. Mom was in so much pain that her medication was useless. We rushed her to the hospital.

On the way I phoned Brice. He assured me he would get there as soon as possible. My mom and I were in the backseat of the car, and I held her the whole way to the hospital. Dad drove in silence, with a worried look on his face.

By the time Brice met us at the hospital Mom had been sedated and was able to rest comfortably. When the doctor came to the waiting room, he told us she would sleep for several hours. Her condition was declining, and there was nothing we could do but wait. We had the option of doing so at home but chose to stay there.

The waiting room was cold and impersonal and the chairs were hard, but we fell asleep nevertheless from emotional exhaustion. I awoke early the next morning and made my way toward Mom's room. The door was cracked, and Dad was inside with her. I was getting ready to go in, but the sound of his voice made me pause. I strained to hear what was going on between them but stayed behind the door.

"Juanita, I don't feel like I have anything to apologize to you for," Dad said.

Mom's voice was faint, so I had to strain to hear her. "I'm not asking for an apology. I just want you to know that I recognize that you've misused me for years. I deserved better and should have left you years ago."

"Why are you saying this now?"

"I should've said something sooner."

"I know we've grown apart, but I never stopped loving you."

Mom didn't respond.

"What's the problem here, Juanita?"

"The abuse, Smitty, the disrespect."

"I know I was wrong for all the times I hit you, but I stopped, didn't I?" He grabbed her hand. "Please don't do this to me right now. It's hard enough watching you slowly leave me."

"Umph . . . even on my deathbed, I still have to cater to your sorry ass."

"What's gotten into you, woman? I don't care how sick you are, you don't have no right to speak to me like that," he said. "I am still your husband."

"The funny thing is that you never did act like a husband," Mom said emphatically. Dad got up and was headed out the door. I stepped back to make sure he didn't see me.

"Her name is Carolyn, and she lives in a high-rise condo downtown, which you purchased for her," Mom said.

My mouth dropped. I had figured Daddy was cheating, but I'd never known the details.

"What are you talking about?" My father turned back to her. "I don't have to listen to this."

"I'm not finished, Smitty. Sit down."

"You're overstepping your boundaries, Juanita."

"Sit down!" Mom said sternly. "You have treated me more like a maid than a wife. You abused me physically, and once you got tired of using your fists, you began hurting me with your words. You have been a poor example to your children, and you act like you could care less. And as if that weren't enough humiliation, you just had to have another woman."

My dad didn't say a word.

"And the sad part about it is that I should have left you a long time ago."

"But you stayed. I must have been doing something right," he had the nerve to say.

"Yes, I stayed, and that is my fault. I did have a choice, and I chose wrong."

"So what are you complaining about?" Dad asked sarcastically.

"Nothing, Smitty. Not a thing. I just want to let you know that I forgive you for everything you've ever done to me and your kids. I'm forgiving you because you don't know any better."

"You finished?" he asked.

"No, I'm not," she said, then paused, struggling to breathe deeply. "I thought about divorcing you. But what good would that do me now? I'm going to be leaving soon anyway. So we'll be apart. I only want to let you know that you no longer control me. I have released myself from the hold you've had over me all these years. I am my own person. And if I am my own person on this earth, if only for one more day or a few months, I am lighter, and free from you."

"You think I care about all that talk?" he said, folding his arms and turning his head away from her.

"I know you don't, Smitty. And it's okay. It doesn't matter to me anymore. I'm prepared for my destiny. Will you be when your time comes?"

He didn't respond.

"You're the only one who has to be accountable for your life," she said. "I've found my peace. I only hope you'll find yours."

He jumped out of his seat like he was about to explode, then he put his hands around her throat. "I'll take you out right now," he threatened.

"I'm leaving anyway, Smitty. Go ahead, do it!"

Just when I started to push the door open to save my mother, Dad fell back in his chair, covered his face with his hands, and began to weep. "Don't die on me, Juanita," he cried. "Not now."

Grief-stricken, he laid his head on the bed beside her. Mom sighed, then put her hand in his.

I stood in the doorway weeping along with my dad.

Mom was leaving us, and Dad was genuinely grieving, but he hadn't changed. Nevertheless, that morning her words had forced him to look at himself and be responsible for his actions. She gave him something to think about, words that I hoped would haunt him long after her time on this earth.

.   .   .   .

My mother died the next day, shortly after we shared a conversation that would forever influence my life.

"Nina, I hope you can find it in your heart to forgive me for teaching you wrong."

"Mom, you've been a wonderful mother to me," I assured her.

"I'm talking about the way I allowed myself to be treated by your father. Just because I accepted it, it didn't make it right."

"I understand." She was weak, and I didn't want to stress her any further. So I kept my comments brief.

"That's the problem, you shouldn't understand. Promise me you'll stay as far away as possible from Maurice, or anybody like him."

"I will," I assured her.

"I'm serious, Nina. He's not good enough for you. You deserve better. Promise me that you won't accept anything less."

"I won't," I said. I put my arms around her and hugged her in what would be our last embrace. I didn't want to let go. I said a silent prayer for her and for me, thanking God for her life and for the words of strength she'd just shared with me.

"Now go get your brother and his wife so I can speak with them," she said, and kissed me on the forehead.

"Okay," I said, and kissed her on the cheek. "I love you, Mom."

When we returned to her room, she wasn't breathing and her eyes were closed. Brice wrapped his arms around her and wept.

"Come back and say bye to me," he cried. "Please, Mom, come back and say bye."

Brianna wrapped her arms around him.

I was in a fog. Nothing about that moment seemed real. I don't remember who pressed the nurses' button, but immediately the nurse ran in and called for additional help. We were asked to leave the room. I remember the three of us clinging to one another as we made our way out to the waiting area.

Then it was a reality. Mom was dead. It was a sorrowful time. I kept going over our last conversation. And as sad as I was for me and my brother, I had a sense that she was fine with what happened to her. Although her life hadn't been ideal, she had lived her dream of raising a family. Her oldest son was accomplished and had married a good woman. Before she died, she shared with me words it took her a lifetime to understand and accept for herself. She had even made peace with her husband's treatment of her. I only wished she could have been around longer to enjoy her newfound freedom, but I found solace knowing and understanding her state of awakening, however brief. I knew that last conversation encompassed all that she ever wanted for me but didn't always know how to say. She did want what was best for me. She wanted me to live a full, happy life. My gift to her would be to do so.

A New Day

Twenty-eight

After my mom's death, time seemed to fly. Two months had gone by, and Thanksgiving was around the corner. Brice and I had grown closer. I spent a lot of time at his and Brianna's new house, sometimes staying entire weekends. I needed to feel close to them, and they seemed to understand. But we grew apart from our dad. When I did stay there in the house with him, he wasn't home much. When he was, we only said what was necessary to live under the same roof. He was grieving in his own way, but I couldn't relate to his process, and he couldn't relate to mine.

Brice and I were caught off guard when Dad called a family meeting. We hadn't had one of those since Brice was in high school, so we were sure he had an important announcement. He didn't let on what he was going to speak with us about and kept his distance from me all day until Brice showed up.

We sat in the living room and began the meeting by attempting small talk. Even with all of us present, the house seemed empty.

"So, how's it going over at the spa?" Dad asked Brice.

"Going good. I'm beginning to remodel. I'm going to expand the spa area and make it more inviting for the ladies. I'm decreasing the stylist area and moving it to another part of the building. I think it'll be classier that way."

"Are you sure that's a good idea, son?" Dad asked.

"I saw the plans; it's going to be a good move," I said.

"Maybe you should let me take a look at those plans," he said.

"That's cool," Brice replied. "So, why did you call the meeting, Dad?" He seemed restless being there in the house, eager to get to Dad's purpose.

"Well, son, Nina, I've decided to sell the house," he announced.

"You want to do *what*?" I yelled.

"There's no need in keeping it," he said.

"Where are you going to move to?" I asked. I couldn't wait to hear his answer. I knew he wasn't going to move into another house.

"Downtown," he replied.

"What? You're buying a condo?" Brice asked sarcastically. I had already told him about the conversation I overheard between Mom and him. Brice told me he'd had an idea that Dad was playing around but didn't know there was one woman in particular.

"No. Actually, I'm going to move in with a lady friend of mine," he said matter-of-factly.

At this point nothing that my dad did surprised me. I was hurt by his decision, but he had to live his life and I knew that what I thought or what my brother thought wouldn't influence him. But I had to express my opinion. "I think you're wrong," I said.

"I disagree," he said.

"So why are you wasting our time telling us?" Brice asked.

"As if our opinion mattered," I added.

"Dad, I know you're a grown man, and you have a right to make your own decisions," Brice said. "You didn't have to call a meeting—you could have just told me this over the phone." He got up and headed toward the foyer, then came back.

My father said, "I wanted to let you two know because I'm going to need some help cleaning out the house and finding a charity to give your mother's things to."

I wanted to walk away from him too. He didn't even give the dirt on Mom's casket time to settle before he ran to his mistress. I looked at him, and for the first time I realized he was a weak, pitiful man. I was disgusted that he was my father.

Brice said, "Dad, I can't help, man. I'm gonna be too busy with the remodeling."

"Now don't you get so big that you forget who gave you the money to get that business started."

"I haven't forgotten, Dad, but to be honest, I can't help you disrespect my mother. This move makes me wonder how you truly felt about her, but I loved her and still do." Brice turned to look Dad directly in the eye. "I can't help you treat her death so casually. I'm sorry, but you're on your own." He walked out of the house.

Dad got up to follow him but changed his mind. "I'll be in the basement," he said, and walked past me. I knew my opinion didn't matter to him.

But I felt miserable. I wasn't prepared for yet another change. I had gone through too much. I had graduated, moved, moved again, then yet again. I had gone through an abusive, unhealthy relationship and allowed the only man who ever truly cared about me to get away. I had buried my mom. I was holding on to my job by a thread because of all of the changes I'd experienced. My dad was not about to force me to have to find another place and move yet again. I knew he was only concerned about himself, but I was concerned about myself, too, and moving would have been the last straw.

"I'm not leaving," I said.

"Don't start with me," he shot back.

"I'm not leaving!"

"You can stay until the house is sold, but after that you need to get a place."

"I'm staying, because I'm buying this house," I said before I could stop myself. Then I became confident with my decision. "That's right, I'm buying this house."

"Nina, stop playing games. You can't afford this house. Not with your salary."

"Then you give it to me," I said.

"Are you crazy? At this point, the family meeting is over. End of discussion. I'm calling the Realtor first thing Monday," he said, and walked out of the living room.

Although my dad was out of listening range, I repeated aloud to myself, "I'm going to buy this house, and you can't stop me!"

Twenty-nine

After enduring a lengthy phone conversation in which I screamed, yelled, and cried about my dad, Janelle agreed to come over and console me.

While I waited for her to arrive, I found myself walking through every square foot of the house. Most nights I stayed there alone. When Dad did stay, he either dozed off on the sofa in the basement or slept in Brice's old room. After Mom died, he never slept in their room again. That night I was alone, and for the first time, it felt eerie. There was an unsettled feeling in the house. I wasn't sure if it was me, or my mom's displeasure over what was happening with her family.

As I walked through each room, I turned on a light, and by the time I got to my parents' room every light in the house was on. I hesitantly opened the door and walked in but I couldn't bring myself to turn on the light switch. My mother was in the room—I felt her. The closer I got to her side of the bed, where she had lain helpless just months ago, the more intensely I felt her presence. Entranced, I picked up one of her pillows and smelled it. Her scent was still there. Overwhelmed, I fell to my knees and began to weep. I whispered, "Mom, help me! I need you. Please help me!"

I so deeply needed her guidance. I didn't know which way to turn or what my next move would need to be, and I missed her so terribly. I needed her to reappear and be there for me. Squeezing my eyes shut, I prayed to God to bring my mother back to me, or at least give me a sign that she wanted me to keep her house. Maybe I was being selfish in my decision. Maybe she wanted me to move on, away from my home.

At some point after sobbing and praying to God and Mom, I finally ran out of words and thoughts. I remained there on my knees, hearing only my breath. It was so quiet that I could scarcely hear my heart beating.

Following the lingering silence came peace.

I knew that everything was going to be okay. That I had every right to want my mother's house, and although I wasn't sure how, I knew I was going to be able to keep it. I moved off my knees and sat on the recliner. I looked around at my mother's room, at the pictures and keepsakes she had collected through the years. This place deserved to have a new energy moving through its walls. And my mother deserved to have her offspring feel peace in this house, a peace she couldn't have for herself.

I don't know how much time had passed when I finally realized the doorbell was ringing. I snapped back to reality, looking around to make sure I had heard right. It chimed again, double time, and I ran to answer the door.

"What took you so long?" Janelle asked. "I've been out here at least five minutes."

"Are you serious?"

"At least two, but that's too long." She softened her approach. "Are you okay, honey?" I'm sure under typical circumstances she wouldn't have sugarcoated her words, but I'm glad she did now.

"Better now that you're here." We embraced.

"Good," she replied, and followed me into the kitchen. "You got anything to eat?"

Normally people are weird around their friends following the loss of a loved one. They're awkward and don't quite know what to say, but not Janelle. And I was loving her at that moment for her ability to continue being herself, despite my loss.

"What you got a taste for?" I asked.

"Anything that your mother—" she began, then caught herself. "Sorry about that."

"Don't apologize," I said. "I sometimes forget that she's gone myself. How about some cold cuts and chips?"

Instead of wallowing in her mistake, Janelle allowed the conversation to move forward. "Girl, that sounds good to me. Chips in the pantry?"

"Yeah."

"I'll get 'em. Now tell me more about wanting to buy this house."

"Not wanting to. I'm going to."

We sat at the table preparing our sandwiches. While I explained to her my reasons for wanting the house, I was struck with the idea to go through our family's files.

Janelle was just about to take a bite of her sandwich when I abruptly announced, "Let's take our sandwiches to the basement. We can eat and look."

"Look for what?" she asked.

"I'm not sure, but I want to go through my family's papers. I just feel like there might be something there that could help me."

"Okay . . ." Janelle reluctantly replied, and picked up her plate and the bag of chips and followed me.

The basement included a TV area, a full bath, an extra bedroom, and a room that acted as an office/family-files storage room. Inside was a desk with an older-model computer that was seldom used. In the corner, left of the desk, was a four-drawer file cabinet with a stack of filing boxes next to it.

I had never taken the time to go through all our old papers, mostly tax returns and receipts, medical records, and bank and investment statements. I couldn't pinpoint what I was looking for, but my gut was pushing me to search for anything that could possibly help me in my quest to buy the house.

Janelle tried to appear enthusiastic, but after a half hour of looking for something that seemed to not be there, she ran out of steam, especially after several unsuccessful attempts at conversation with me. I can't explain what was going on with me, but it was as if I was in a trance. I'm sure my mother's spirit was guiding me, or maybe it was God. I didn't want to think about anything else until I got my answer.

"So, have you spoken with Leo?" she asked.

I didn't answer.

She raised her voice. "Nina, has Leo called?"

"Uh, yeah," I replied. "He called a few days after the funeral."

"What did he say?" she asked.

"He extended his condolences." I closed one drawer of the file cabinet and opened the next.

She sighed.

"What about Maurice?"

"Yeah."

"He called?" she asked, startled.

"Yeah."

"When?"

"Sometime last week."

"What did he say?" She stopped looking at the papers and gave me her full attention.

"Extended his condolences."

I could tell she was becoming restless, so I suggested she go up-stairs and bring us down cookies and milk. That seemed to bring her back to life. She quickly got up and dashed out of the office and up the stairs.

I had gotten to one of the last file folders in the bottom drawer of the cabinet. It was labeled JUANITA LANDER.

When Janelle returned with cookies and milk on a tray, I was going through its contents.

"Girl, did you leave every light on in the house?" she asked. "I turned some of them off."

I looked up at Janelle with a smile of content and relief, because I had discovered exactly what I had been looking for.

Thirty

I began the workweek a new woman brimming with energy. It was the beginning of the holiday season, and the commercials and streets reflected the spirit of celebration. The average person was probably coasting through the workday, mentally winding down for the holiday parties and festivities to come. I, on the other hand, had moved into a zone. I wanted to work, to prove myself. I hadn't been with the station for a full year yet, and I hadn't proven my strength or ability to grow as a reporter.

My first order of business was to meet with the producer to set personal goals, and to make sure the grace that he had extended to me to stick with my job was still there.

"Nina, you're just the person I wanted to see," he said.

"Yes, sir," I said. I became a bit nervous, because I didn't know what to expect. My first thought was that he wanted to let me go.

"Come on, let's go into my office," he said. I followed him inside and took a seat across from his desk.

I decided to speak first and plead my case, hoping that maybe he would change his mind before he could fire me.

"May I say something before you tell me your news?" I asked.

"Okay. Go ahead."

"This position is important to me, and I intend to work hard and prove that the station made the right choice in hiring me. I know my performance can stand improvement, but I'm ready to step up to the plate and prove myself." I spoke with as much confidence as I could muster.

"Good. That means you will be willing to take on some extra assignments during the holidays, right?"

"Right," I said.

"It'll mean working longer hours and some weekends. I hope you'll be up to that because our polls have shown that our audience enjoys seeing and hearing you report about what goes on around this city."

"Really?"

"Nina, I know it's been tough losing your mother," he said. "I lost my father to a heart attack nearly three years ago, and I still miss him. You'll make it through, I guarantee it."

I was grateful for his words.

"Gus has agreed to continue covering with you, and the three of us will meet later this week to discuss the additions to your schedule."

"Thank you," I replied.

He looked down at his papers, indicating that our meeting was over, so I got up and turned to leave.

"Miss Lander," he called from behind me. I stopped and turned around. "I don't say this to everyone, so don't take my words too lightly."

"What is it?" I asked.

"If you continue to grow and work hard, and I'm sure you will, you have the talent to one day make a fine anchor."

I nearly lost my breath. I so desperately needed those words on that day and at that moment. "Thank you, sir. Thank you."

"But you're going to have to work hard to get there, so you'd better be getting your day started."

"Yes sir," I replied, and rushed out of his office. I couldn't wait to tell Gus that Nina was back!

Thirty-one

Over the next few weeks the Realtor paraded individuals, couples, and whole families through my house. Dad was seldom around during the showings, and I was usually at work, so I wasn't quite sure how the prospects were looking until I received a call one evening from Dad.

I had just taken a load of clothes out of the dryer and had positioned myself in front of the television. It had been a while since I'd had the opportunity to sit down and watch a good football game or sitcom, and I was looking forward to some entertainment.

"Hey, Nina, how's it going?" he asked as if we had been consistently in touch and shared nothing but warm feelings for each other.

"I'm cool, just folding clothes and looking at a game."

"Who's playing?" he asked.

"Falcons in St. Louis against the Rams. It should be a good game."

"St. Louis, my old stomping grounds. Maybe I should hurry home to see it."

Although I was extremely angry at my father, I was glad that he'd be watching the game with me. I felt sorry for him that he couldn't be a better person, but I did love him. The thought of us watching the game together reminded me of old times when Brice and I would sit around with him watching basketball or football.

Before I could stop myself, I said, "Do you want me to pop some popcorn?"

"Huh?" he asked.

"Oh, when you said home, you didn't mean here. My bad, Daddy."

"Oh, I didn't know what you were talking about," he awkwardly chuckled.

That stung. I had let my guard drop. I didn't want that feeling, but it was there. I had almost forgotten I was in a real dilemma with my dad and that it would probably take a lot for us to be able to sit down and watch a game together. I was overcome with the unsettling feeling that it might never happen again.

"Well, I called to let you know that we found a buyer for the house," he said.

"Really," I said casually.

"Yeah, I know tomorrow is Thanksgiving, but we need to get together sometime this weekend to discuss finalizing everything. Could you call your brother so you two can decide if Saturday or Sunday would be better? I'd prefer Sunday."

"You're right, we do need to have a discussion," I said.

"So, what are you doing for Thanksgiving?" he asked.

"As if you care," I said underneath my breath. "Oh, I have plans." I had planned to spend the day reporting the local and sports news, then join Brice and Brianna for dinner, but I chose not to let him know.

"Good. Try to let me know what Brice says by Friday, okay?"

"Gotcha," I replied, acting unfazed by his indifference.

The old me would probably have gotten off the phone, run to my room, and bawled myself to sleep. But not this Nina. I hung up, folded the rest of my clothes, popped some popcorn for myself, and enjoyed the rest of the football game. And it was a close one—the Falcons nearly lost, but they pulled through.

I found comfort in knowing that although it was too late to save my daddy—because he didn't want to be saved or I just plain didn't know how—I had the opportunity to save myself from the heartache and pain that my family had somehow inherited.

Brice had already begun the steps of change. That evening it became imperative that I stick by my plan to stop being a victim and join my brother in breaking the vicious cycle that had entangled each of us and killed my mom. From that day forward, I pledged to prove to my mother and my father that I could remain strong, victorious.

Thirty-two

We were set to meet Daddy late Sunday afternoon. That morning I attended church with Brice and Brianna. The sermon—on the topic of strength and courage—was informative and timely. The minister said, "Do not be discouraged, for the Lord will be with you wherever you go." His words stuck with me all the way to the house, as I sat in the backseat of Brice's car. I repeated them and held them close to my spirit because that evening I was going to go where no female Lander had ever gone, head-to-head with Smitty Lander.

At home Brianna, Brice, and I settled in, then moved into the kitchen to prepare brunch. We had two hours to fill our stomachs and relax before Dad would arrive. I had prepared Brice, over Thanksgiving dinner, for my plan to buy the house. He assured me that he'd be by my side and do whatever he could to make sure I got it.

It was a pleasure to see Brice working in the kitchen. Brianna was a good teacher, and he was awkward but enthusiastic, and I admired their closeness. As they worked together slicing up a melon, the telephone rang. I almost didn't want to answer it because the moment was picture-perfect. It made me realize that I longed for a relationship with someone who had a mutual fondness for me.

I picked up. "Hello!"

"Is this Nina?"

"Yes, it is."

"Hi, Nina. How are you? It's been so long since we talked."

"Who is this?"

"Oh, sorry. I figured you would have recognized my voice."

"Well, I don't," I said, agitated. I had enough things to think about without having to figure out who was on the other end of the phone.

"Did I catch you at a bad time?"

"It depends on who . . ." It finally clicked. I knew the voice on the other end of the line, and no, I wasn't too busy to speak to him. I was elated that he had called. I hadn't expected to hear from Leo again after his courtesy call following my mother's funeral. I felt guilty for the way I had conducted myself in our relationship, so calling him was out of the question. "Hi!" I chimed.

"Oh, so you do know who you're speaking with."

"Yes I do. So how are you, Mr. LJ Love? I am so proud of what you've accomplished with your new album, and the remix version of your latest single just takes your vibe to another level."

"Wow, I wasn't expecting to hear such a warm greeting from you."

I didn't respond. Maybe I did overdo it, but I was proud of him, and so glad to be speaking with him.

"Not that I mind," he said. "It's good to know you've been keeping up, especially because I figured you weren't feeling me anymore."

I had left things unresolved between us, and I knew Leo wasn't the type of person who would force the issue, but I owed it to him and myself to properly apologize. Only I didn't know where to begin.

"Well, happy holidays. How was your Thanksgiving?" he asked.

"Nice. I had to work. How was yours? Did you spend it with your mom?"

"She's in Asia. I went with a group of friends to North Carolina and hung out near an Indian reservation. We spent the weekend being social and gambling. I just got back early this morning."

"Sounds like you had a good time."

"Well, we wanted to speak with the Native Americans and get a feel for how they perceived the whole Thanksgiving celebration. But I'll tell you about that some other time. Right now I wanna ask you a question."

"Before you go any further, Leo, my dad is on his way over and we're about to have an important family discussion. Would you have a problem with us talking some other time?"

"Oh, my bad," he said defensively.

"No, I apologize that I have to be so short. I'm really glad you called. I think we need to talk. Can we schedule some time to meet? I have a full week, but maybe we can get together late next Saturday or Sunday afternoon."

"What about later this Sunday?" he asked. "How long do you think your meeting will be?" Leo never played games. When he said he wanted to see me, he meant it. There was no wavering. I liked that about him.

I hated to seem uninterested, but I just didn't know what would take place at the meeting. "I'm not sure. But why don't I call you afterward and we'll go from there?"

"Okay, Nina. I look forward to hearing from you."

"Leo, thanks for calling, sincerely."

"No problem."

•   •   •   •

Dad arrived. "Hey, everybody," he said, announcing himself as he made his way down to the basement to join us. We were watching football. I can't remember who was playing, because my mind hadn't been on the game. Dad looked at least five years younger, wearing a leather jacket, an all-leather baseball hat, and shades. The air that he carried with him made me sick. He seemed to be on top of the world. A world where nobody seemed to matter but himself.

He smiled, removed his shades, and asked, "Who's playing?"

I cringed. Brice answered him, while I began to focus on just how I was going to state my case to him.

"So, is it one that you could bear to break away from?" he asked.

Brice, who was snuggled on the sofa with Brianna, reached for the remote control and muted the volume.

"Okay then, let's get down to business. Nina, you didn't happen to cook anything, did you?"

"No," I answered. And I wasn't about to either. Not for him.

"I sure could use something good to eat, but I guess I'll have to wait."

"You want some chips?" Brice asked, picking up a bowl off the table and attempting to pass it to him.

"No thanks. It'll ruin my appetite," he replied, taking his favorite seat in the basement, the recliner. "Well, there are several reasons that I wanted to meet today. As you all already know, we have a serious buyer for the house."

I couldn't hold back my attitude—it leaped out. "Make that two."

"Now, Nina, you don't still have that crazy idea of wanting to buy the house, do you?"

"Like I said, we have two buyers." I couldn't believe how bold and blatant I was being, but it was the only way I knew to handle the situation.

"Anyway. I just need you two to sign your names on this form and everything will be taken care of." He placed a document on the table, reached into his jacket pocket, and pulled out a pen, which he put neatly beside it. Then he proudly announced, "And Nina, the new buyers said they'd even give you thirty days to find a new place. Maybe you could move back into your old loft. It was nice."

"I don't want to waste money renting anymore."

"I know, but I decided that after everything is finalized, I'm going to pay your rent up for the year, so this won't be as big of a strain as it could be."

"Dad, I appreciate your offer. I think it's very generous, but I want to buy the house. And you know that I can."

"What are you talking about?" he asked. "I'm offering you a good deal. Be smart."

"I was hoping you'd come clean, but I guess I have to tell you what you already know." I sat up in my chair. "Dad, you and Mom put the house in Brice's and my name the week after I graduated from college so that we wouldn't have to pay an inheritance tax if something were to happen to you and Mom."

"Yeah, you're right. That's why I need you two to sign these papers."

"Dad, part of the house is mine and I'm not signing."

"Yes, the house is in your names, but I'm the one who worked hard to pay off the mortgage. Why should I just let you have the house? You didn't put a dime into it." He was angry.

I sat back and listened to him. He was right, I didn't pay the mortgage. "But I'm not asking you to give me the house. I'm just asking you to work out a deal with me."

He huffed, and sat back in his seat. "Nina, I don't believe you're going against me like this. Your own father." He shook his head. "Your mother would turn over in her grave if she knew you were being so malicious."

After an awkward silence, Brianna said, "Maybe I shouldn't be down here. I think I'm just going to go upstairs."

Nobody said anything. She stood up.

"No, baby, I think you need to stay," Brice said, and motioned for her to sit. "This is your family now, too. Dad, I'd like to have seen you and Nina work this out between yourselves, but I want her to have this house too. We should keep it in the family, and if she wants the responsibility, why shouldn't she have it?"

"You too?" Dad said. He stood up. "This conversation is over. You two are conspiring against me, your own dad."

"Oh, so you're just going to walk away?" I said.

"If I don't walk away, I can't be responsible for what I might say."

"But you weren't so careful about your word choices with Mom," Brice said. "What makes us any different?" My mouth dropped. He had stood up to Daddy.

"Both of you have lost your minds," Dad said.

I could see the anger swelling up in Brice's face. "If you got something to say, we're here. Say it!" he said as calmly as he could.

"Both of you are just like your mother. She never did understand me, and neither do you," he said, and began walking toward the stairs.

"But did that give you a reason to beat her?" Brice asked.

Dad stopped dead in his tracks. "When was the last time you saw me hit your momma?"

I wanted to go off, but I allowed Brice to step to the plate, be the beautiful man he had become, and release what he was feeling. "Daddy, you never stopped beating Momma until the day she died. You beat her with your words, until she couldn't take it anymore. And Dad, I hate to say this, but even though I didn't want to see Mom go, I prefer knowing she's with the Lord than having to live under your constant torment."

"Boy, do you think that I didn't love your mother?" he said. There was silence, and he walked back toward the chair. I was expecting him to say something that would give me insight on his behavior all those years. I think we all were. "Y'all don't know what really went on. It wasn't as bad as she made it to be. I provided for your momma and both of you. What more could I have given her?"

"Love, Daddy. You could have given her love," I said.

"Nina, you're too young to even know what love is," he said. He reached over and snatched the document off the table, stood up, tore it into pieces, and said, "Take the damn house, Nina. At this point I don't care what y'all do!" Then he stormed up the stairs.

Brice looked at me, stunned.

What just happened? I asked myself.

I wasn't sure if I had won or lost.

Thirty-three

I awoke the next morning out of a weird dream. I dreamt that Momma was trapped in the house, and I was trying to get to her to save her. Daddy was guarding the door and wouldn't let me inside. I pleaded with him to open the door, but he wouldn't.

I grudgingly got dressed and left for work early, but I couldn't shake the emotions that the dream provoked.

It was a long day at work, but I managed to make it through. I wasn't back in the comfort of my home until after 11:00 P.M. I was aching inside and wanted to talk to someone. It occurred to me that I hadn't returned Leo's call the previous night because I was too distraught over my family's situation. But I needed to see him. After pacing around in the kitchen, I gathered the courage to call.

"Hi, Leo," I said, attempting to be upbeat.

"Hey, Nina."

"What are you doing?" I asked.

"Just chillin' out."

"Do you want to do that over here?" I asked.

"Excuse me?"

"Do you want to chill out over here with me?" I boldly asked.

"You do know what time it is, don't you? And don't you have to be up early in the morning?"

"Yes to all of that, but Leo, I really need to be in your company right now." I wanted to explain myself but decided to let my request stand as it was.

He hesitated, but in true form he didn't pretend that he didn't want to see me. He simply replied, "Okay, I'll be right over."

.　.　.　.

Leo arrived at midnight. I had almost forgotten just how wonderful it was to be in his company.

There was an awkward silence between us when he first walked through the door. But after we hugged, I remembered every special thing about him. I felt so at ease. Very few men have given me the feeling of complete security, but with him it always seemed like everything would turn out for the good, no matter what. Just having him there in the house with me gave me a sense of relief. I had missed everything about him—his dreads, his scent, his calm demeanor.

We cozied ourselves in the basement and flipped through the channels for whatever seemed interesting. After finding a suitable program, I put down the remote and focused my attention on Leo. Before I could say anything he spoke.

"I know there are things that we need to talk about, but we don't have to do that tonight, if you don't want to," he said. "We can always have that discussion another time. Whatever you need from me tonight, I'm here to offer it."

I didn't want a deep discussion. As a matter of fact, I didn't want to talk at all. I just wanted to be with him. For the first time, I truly appreciated him, and I realized that I wanted to somehow incorporate him into my everyday life. Even if he didn't want to try to restore what we once had, I hoped we'd at least be able to be friends.

"I just want you to hold me," I said.

We spent the remainder of the evening just being close. Very few words were exchanged, but the vibe between us was one of knowing. Knowing that when we were ready to talk, our words would be mature and we would use the time to move our relationship forward. I also knew he wouldn't place blame but would hear me out and make a fair decision.

We eventually turned off the TV and went up to my room, where we wrapped ourselves in each other's arms. I felt at home.

Maybe my father was right—with Maurice I didn't understand the meaning of love. I had always thought it meant that I had to fight hard for what I wanted, or that it was the feeling at the pit of my stomach that propelled me to do whatever it took, no matter how crazy, to obtain affection.

But being with Leo and feeling his calm in the midst of my personal storm helped me to better understand love. I grasped that it is unconditional, it is nonjudgmental, it is offered without force. It's like that old saying, "If you love something, let it go. If it comes back to you, it's true love; if it never returns, it was never yours after all."

Maybe my mom should have let my father go, and maybe he should have let her go, instead of living a life of daily heartache. I realized that I was walking in their footsteps by fighting for the house. It was only further hurting my father, and it didn't make me feel any better. I loved myself, and, no matter how cruel he was, I loved my father, enough to stop reciprocating the abuse. So I gave up the fight then and there. And surrendered to everything that I felt bitter about: my mom dying, my dad not changing for the better, my restlessness.

"Thank you," I whispered.

"For what?" Leo asked.

"For just being you," I replied.

I closed my eyes and dozed off. It was the most peaceful sleep I'd had since my mother had passed.

. . . .

That night I dreamt of a couple. I couldn't see their faces, but they were holding hands and walking on a beach. I watched them closely. They ended up in a boat. The man was rowing, and the woman was sitting behind him hugging him tightly. The calm water began to rage out of control, but the man kept paddling forward. The woman never let go of him, and never once seemed afraid. As they were about to get swallowed by a wave, a strong wind came from the opposite direction and the water calmed. The man turned to look at the woman, who never let him go.

Epilogue

It was New Year's Eve. Leo and I were there because I wanted to celebrate with my close friends, family, and a few members of the press. I wanted to celebrate all of our accomplishments over the past year. When I first met Leo, I naïvely dismissed him. But we were adults now, standing around in good company and good cheer. Brice and Brianna were there together. Brianna was five months' pregnant, and the expectant couple was passing around their ultrasound pictures. Brice bragged that his son would be a super entrepreneur, just like his father. Brianna said that their daughter would be an accomplished pianist. After debating back and forth, they finally agreed that whatever the sex of the baby, they just wanted it to be healthy.

Janelle and Tim were there. They had gotten engaged the previous New Year but hadn't settled on a date to tie the knot. She chose dates during the baseball seasons that were impossible to make work, and he chose dates that conflicted with what Janelle thought was the perfect wedding weather. Janelle would complete her master's in business administration in the spring. She and Brice, of all people, were planning a partnership after her graduation. They planned to expand his spa into a chain throughout the South.

She was looking as glamorous as ever. I had just given the two of them the grand tour of the house, and we had joined the rest of the party down in the basement. The decorations were elegant, Mom's favorite color: lavender. The entire gang, including Daddy, had spent any bit of our free time throughout the year remodeling and redecorating, and put extra effort into implementing the party arrangements.

"We did a good job," Janelle said. "Juanita would be proud."

"I think she is proud!" I replied.

Brice and I would never again have the same relationship with Dad, but we were on speaking terms with him and couldn't help but respect all the efforts he had put toward the house. We were not at all interested in being around his new wife, but he brought her to the celebration with him anyway. We didn't resist, because despite his faults, and though we had a lot of forgiving yet to do, we still loved him. He wasn't going to do much changing, but he was still our father.

"Nina, it's time," Gus said.

I walked to the microphone that was set up at the front of the room.

"I want to thank you all for coming out this evening," I began. "This is such a special night, and what better way to celebrate the new year than by giving back to our community."

There was applause.

"My mother, Juanita Lander, was a special woman. She was a loyal mother and wife, who devoted her entire existence to her family. Although she may not have always received the same in return," I said, and looked up at my dad.

More applause.

"Although she is no longer with us, her life was not in vain. A good number of people in this room have seen to it that Juanita Lander's memory will live on forever. With the creation of the Juanita Lander House for Battered Women, those women in Atlanta who experience the heartache of living with an abusive spouse will now have a place of refuge."

"There are so many people I would like to thank. First I would like to thank a very dear friend, Ms. Clara Jones." The group clapped, and Leo's mom raised her hand, smiled and waved. Then she blew me a kiss, which I returned.

"It was Clara's idea to transform the home that I grew up in into a gift for others." I paused. "I would also like to thank everyone who helped make the project become a reality. A lot of hard work and sweat went into this house. Including my dad, Mr. Smitty Lander." Dad froze. I don't think he wanted any attention on him. "And my brother, Brice Lander. You and Brianna have been invaluable."

"I'd also like to thank Cindy and Junie for their donation. Both of you do so much for the city of Miami, I appreciate your extending your generosity to our community and for taking time out of your busy schedules to spend your New Year's here with us."

They nodded.

I continued down my list of thank-yous and included Janelle, Tim, and some of his teammates, Gus, my old boss, many of my new friends through Leo, and old work associates.

"Last, but definitely not least, I would like to acknowledge someone who is very special to me. When the house went on the market a second time, knowing how special it was to me, he purchased it. You all know him as LJ Love, but I simply call him Leo."

The crowd clapped and looked around to see where he was standing, but none of us could find him. Silence fell over the room.

"Leo, where are you?" I asked.

"Here I come," he yelled, descending the stairs.

Everyone turned to see Leo emerge with a bouquet of roses. They were red, pink, white, yellow. He walked through the crowd to the front of the room. Leave it to him to be different.

"Hello, everybody," he said. "Excuse me if I appear a bit nervous, but I'm about to attempt a feat that I have never before tried." Everyone laughed. He looked over at me. I could tell he was up to something mischievous.

"These are for you," he said, and placed the roses in my hands.

"All of you who know Nina well must know that she's an incredible woman. And not just because you will soon be seeing her every night on *CNN Sports Center*, and not because she believed in this project so much that she pushed and pushed until it became a reality. Trust me, I know. I was here between recording sessions.

"She is special to me because I love her and I like who I am when I'm with her, and I hope she feels the same. 'Cause a brother like me needs a good lady in his life, full-time." He went down on one knee. I gulped.

"Nina, I've watched you since my freshman year in high school. Recently, I've had the opportunity to see you grow into a beautiful woman. I loved you when I first saw you, and I love you even more now."

I was crying, the happiest tears I'd ever shed.

"Nina, if you want to share your life with a good brother, I will be him. Nina Lander, will you honor me by saying you'll be my wife?" He opened a small wrapped box and presented me with the most beautiful ring I could ever have asked for.

I knew what I wanted, and he was it. I wanted to say yes, but I couldn't speak. I was too choked up. My arms were filled with roses. I didn't know what to do with myself.

"Nina, are you gonna give me an answer?" he said, grinning nervously.

"Yes. I will marry you."

I was so excited that I threw the flowers in the air. Roses went everywhere, and our family and friends caught them as they flew. I passionately kissed my new fiancé. Then Leo placed the ring on my finger. I put my arms around him again, and as he held me close, lifting me off my feet, I felt my past, my present, and my future merge. He was my soul mate, and I trusted in our relationship.

I knew that with him my life wouldn't be picture-perfect, but it would be a good life, one absent of deliberate heartache and anguish. Merging with him would mean a new way of loving. And I did love Mr. Leo Jones, a.k.a. LJ Love, and I knew he loved me equally, passionately, truly.

Elated, I looked around at my blessing, having family and friends witness and applaud one of the happiest moments in my life. A sense of peace overcame me. I was certain that all was well with my mother. I could feel her presence with me, and for once I knew she was happy in that house.

Reading Group Guide

1. There are two very different conceptions of marriage in *Hand-me-down Heartache*: the kind Janelle describes, the loving partnership of her parents, and the kind Nina describes, the exploitative and emotionally abusive relationship of her own parents. How common are marriages like these? If these types represent two extremes, do most marriages fall more toward one end or the other?

2. Nina initially discounts Brianna as her brother's latest, but certainly not last, girlfriend. But in some ways, Brianna turns out to be a stronger woman than Nina; she is willing to refuse Brice until she is sure he has changed his destructive behavior. Why can't Nina do the same with Maurice? What does Brianna realize that Nina doesn't?

3. Nina's relationship with Maurice quickly degenerates after the initial romance is over, and even though Maurice manipulates her emotions and cheats on her, Nina takes him back every time. Who is more wrong, Maurice, for his actions, or Nina, for tolerating them? Is their relationship abusive? What role does Nina's self-esteem play in the cycle of their relationship?

4. Leo is different from Maurice in almost every way, and while Nina know he cares for her, she still can't help herself from leaving a good man for a bad one. Only when she achieves peace with herself does she seem ready for Leo. Why is this? Are we unable to have healthy relationships until we are healthy ourselves?

5. The illness and death of her mother is a devastating event in Nina's life, and it is only when confronted with the prospect of losing her mother that she begins to realize what is really important. How does Nina change? Do the same events bring about any change in Nina's father? Why or why not?

6. Like many women in bad relationships, Nina refuses to blame anything on Maurice and attributes most of their problems to her own actions. How can Nina be so perceptive about her parents' relationship but so unwilling to examine her relationship with Maurice in the same way? Are most women more accommodating of their men than they should be?

7. The men in *Hand-me-down Heartache* represent a range of types. Discuss how the men—Brice, Smitty, Leo, and Maurice—differ. How much alike are Maurice and Smitty? If Brice hadn't met Brianna would he have changed?

8. To some extent, Brice and Nina carry the legacy of their par-

ents' marriage to their own relationships. Discuss the effect of this legacy for Nina and Brice. What are the similarities between their relationships and their parents'? How much do we replicate the mistakes of our parents?

9. As a long-suffering wife, Nina's mother, Juanita, rarely challenges her husband. Only after she becomes ill does she confront Smitty with his abusive behavior. Does it matter that Smitty doesn't admit his mistakes? Why does she wait so long? Is it ever too late to change?

10. When friends disagree with one another's choices, they must balance judgment and support to maintain the friendship. Discuss Janelle's friendship with Nina. How well does she manage this balance? When do we follow our friends' advice and when don't we?

An excerpt from Tajuana "TJ"
Butler's hot new novel,

the night before thirty

Alecia, Catara, Elise, Lashawnda, and Tanya are five women who
live in different cities around the country (Los Angeles, New York,
Louisville, Atlanta, and Chicago) and don't know one another—
at least, not yet. But they do have a few things in common: they
all listen to the number one African-American syndicated radio
show, they all have the same birthday, and they are all about to hit
the big 3-0. They meet through a contest sponsored by the radio
show, after which their lives will never be the same. . . .

Sixteen

AND THE WINNERS ARE . . .

*L*ouisa Montero handed the list of winners of the Night Before Thirty contest to Melvin Green.

"How did y'all ever narrow the list down to five?" he asked on the air.

"Believe me, it wasn't easy," she replied. "It's going to be a while before I can read another letter. I'm burnt out."

"That means you're really going to need this birthday getaway," Melvin Green said. Then he announced, "All right, ladies, grab your suitcases and sunscreen and be prepared to meet Louisa Montero in sunny South Beach if your name is called."

· · · ·

Catara closed the door of the dressing room, where her client was trying on clothes. With dresses draped over one arm, she adjusted the volume on her Walkman to make sure she wouldn't miss even one of the names called.

She braced herself for the verdict. She just knew she was going to hear her name. There was no way she couldn't win. She was already packed. If she didn't win, she didn't know what she would do with herself. She had to win because it was the only plan she had for celebrating her birthday.

.   .   .   .

Alecia lay in bed, half asleep, half awake. Louisa had told her that the winners would be announced Monday morning, so she had set her clock radio the previous night to make sure she tuned in.

Even though she knew she had won, she found herself sitting up in bed, wide-eyed. She was excited in anticipation of hearing her name called on the radio. So what—she wouldn't become a famous actress. Hearing her name on the radio would be her fifteen minutes of fame.

.   .   .   .

Allen sat in front of his computer screen, on pins and needles. He could barely concentrate on the flyer he was working on. Once they began talking about the birthday contest, he had to stop working altogether.

With Hattie's help, he'd written a letter to enter Elise in the contest. He wanted to do something special for her. It was a bit drastic, but Allen couldn't garner the courage to let her know that his feelings for her were growing. He was certain that if she could win the contest, knowing that he entered her in it, she would allow him to get closer to her. Maybe in her excitement, she'd do what he couldn't and let him know she cared for him.

.   .   .   .

Tanya, along with three of her coworkers, gathered in the break room and closed the door. Armed with coffee and bagels, the women crowded around a lone portable radio, waiting to see whether Tanya would be flying away for her dream vacation or if they would have to take her out for the usual birthday dinner.

Tanya sat in front of the radio with her eyes tightly shut. Winning this trip meant more to her than she would have ever let on to them. She needed to win this trip as badly as she needed to breathe.

. . . .

Lashawnda dragged herself into the office. Cicely had called her on her cell phone earlier that morning, begging her to come in, not only to work but also to return her car. Lashawnda decided that working for Cicely was still a steady paycheck even though she and Cicely were no longer a couple; she really needed the income. She'd endured worse circumstances.

When she sat at her desk, she instinctively turned on the radio. She looked down and found in front of her a small, nicely wrapped box with a card that read: *Please forgive me—Cicely.*

Lashawnda stared at the box in disbelief. She picked it up and put it in the palm of her hand. It was a small box. *Jewelry,* she thought. Unsure if she would even accept the gift, Lashawnda pulled the string on the bow.

. . . .

Melvin Green read the first name: "Our first winner is a California girl, Alicia Jewel Parker from Los Angeles."

"It's Ah-*lee-cee*-ah, you cornball, Ah-*lee-cee*-ah!" she yelled at the radio, emphasizing the *e* in the pronunciation. Alecia fell back in her bed. She was perturbed. "I never did like him!" she huffed.

. . . .

Melvin Green moved to the next name. "All right, our next winner is from the Midwest—Louisville, Kentucky, home of the Kentucky Derby. Congratulations, Ms. Elise Ross."

Allen was so excited that he nearly fell out of his seat. He picked up the phone to tell Elise that she had won, and then decided a phone call wouldn't be effective enough. He put the receiver down and looked at the computer. He was supposed to be working. *I'm not getting anything done here anyway,* he thought, jumping up, grabbing his coat and keys, and rushing out the door to tell Elise the good news. Telling her she'd just won a vacation for her birthday would put him one step closer to winning her heart.

. . . .

"Winner number three is from the dirty South! Hotlanta to be exact. All you gotta do is hop down one state and begin to celebrate. Lashawnda Davis, congratulations! You're our next winner."

Lashawnda had totally forgotten they would be announcing the winners today. She dropped the gift from Cicely—an ankle bracelet— and her jaw dropped as well. She'd won. She was actually going to be on a plane for the first time. She jumped up and quietly danced around her desk, so as not to disturb Cicely and her client. How would she make it through the rest of the workweek, knowing that come Friday she would be on her way to Florida?

. . . .

"Our next winner is from my hometown. That's right, the Windy City of Chicago. Please believe I know this lady is going to be glad to get a break from the hawk. Put away your fur and pull out your bathing suit because, Tanya Charles, you're winner number four."

Tanya became physically weak. She was glad that she was sitting down—had she been standing, her legs wouldn't have held her up. She'd never won anything before in her life. Her coworkers were jumping up around her and screaming, causing so much commotion that someone opened the door to the break room. The women froze, but it wasn't their boss, so they relaxed.

"Please hold it down," the older lady said, frowning down her nose at them.

"Excuse us," someone replied.

When she closed the door, everyone laughed and went back to a more toned-down celebration. Tanya smiled along with the ladies but inside she felt fear. She was scared. This trip meant her first step in the direction of becoming independent from Chris. When she returned, Chris would be back from Texas and nothing between them would ever be the same again.

. . . .

Catara hung the dresses she'd been holding on the rack beside the dressing-room door. She didn't want anything in her hands. There was one more name left to be called, and she wasn't sure how she'd react, whether hers was called or not. She didn't want to be responsible for paying for damaged merchandise.

"One more name left. I know you ladies out there are anxious to see if you will be the last name on this list, so I'm going to help build the suspense. Can we get a drumroll please?" He pushed the button on his control board to get the effect.

"The final winner of the Night Before Thirty contest—a shopping spree, the Spa in South Beach, and a one-day cruise to the Grand Bahamas—is from the Big Apple! New York. Congratulations, Catara Edwards, you are our final winner."

Catara threw her arms in the air and let out a loud "Yes!" She had known she would win.

Her client opened the door of the dressing room and peeped out. "Did you call me?" she asked.

Catara was so overjoyed that she began sharing her happiness.

"Can you believe it? I just won a trip over the radio. I'm so excited. I won. I really won."

The lady looked at Catara and smiled. "I'm so happy for you," she said. "But while you're celebrating, could I get this dress in an eight?"

"Oh, of course, no problem," Catara said, dancing toward the showroom to get what her client requested.

.   .   .   .

Louisa Montero announced the winners one more time.

"Alecia Jewel Parker, Elise Ross, Lashawnda Davis, Tanya Charles, and Catara Edwards, I will see you ladies this weekend for a thirtieth birthday celebration you won't soon forget."